FOOTPRINTS
Book 4
Strong Southern Women Series

ALI SPOONER

Affinity
Rainbow Publications

2021

ALSO BY ALI SPOONER

Footprints
© 2021 by Ali Spooner

Affinity E-Book Press NZ LTD.
Canterbury, New Zealand

1st Edition

ISBN: 978-1-99-004927-9 (paperback)
ISBN: 978-1-99-004924-8 (EPUB)
ISBN: 978-1-99-004925-5 (PDF)
ISBN: 978-1-99-004926-2 (KINDLE)

Editor: Angela Koenig
Proof Editor: Alexis Smith
Cover Design: Irish Dragon Designs
Production Design: Affinity Publication Services

ACKNOWLEDGMENTS

I want to thank my fans for following my stories, providing great feedback and encouragement. Writing wouldn't be so much fun without you. Thanks to Affinity, Irish Dragon for the cover art, and the team of editors, readers, and publishers who continue to help me grow as a writer. I would also like to thank the ladies of Melsweb.com. Without your encouragement, I would have never begun this journey.

DEDICATION

For Rhonda.

Thanks for giving me the time to create these stories and your support of my writing. Love you, Babes!

TABLE OF CONTENTS

Footprints

Book 4
Strong Southern Women Series

Ali Spooner

PROLOGUE

Sandy St. Angelo, better known as Squirt, was filled with the spirit of her Louisiana bayou home. The slow movement of the water coursed through her veins, and she reveled in the sights and sounds her young senses had grown to love. One of the few things she loved more than their home was her older sister Cam. Sandy, the youngest of the St. Angelo girls, spent every waking moment possible with Cam. Saying Cam was her idol didn't even begin to touch the depth of their relationship. Most young women of Cam's age would have seen Squirt as a pesky younger sibling, but Cam's overwhelming patience with Squirt was remarkable. Instead of chasing her off after the hundredth "why" question, Cam would sit down with her and answer each question as honestly as she could. Cam seemed to sense at an early age that Sandy, much like her, would never permanently leave the bayou.

Sandy lived for the time she spent out on the water with Cam and devoured every ounce of information Cam passed down from their father, Ronny. She was eager to attend Cam's sporting events at which Cam excelled, further ingraining the ideal of worship for Sandy. A much smaller version of her older sister, Sandy was determined to be just like Cam.

When Cam arrived home one day after Sandy started school, she entered the house and found her mother, Camille, waiting for her in the kitchen. She noted the worried look on her mother's face.

"What's wrong?"

Camille wiped a tear from her eye. "Squirt came home from school, tossed her book bag on the couch, and flew out of the house. I only caught a glimpse of her as she ran past me, but I saw blood on her shirt. If I had to venture a guess, I'd say she is out in the treehouse you two built for her. Will you please go check on her?"

Cam wrapped Camille in a warm hug. "Of course, I will."

Cam spied the fresh-baked cookies and grabbed a handful before exiting the back of the house. She walked along the edge of the bayou until the large oak came into view. She and Sandy had built the treehouse several years earlier, and it had become a refuge for Sandy, a place to go and live out her dreams of being a pirate in the bayou. Cam finished off a cookie and then stored the rest in her hoodie's pocket to free her hands for climbing. Sandy wasn't in sight, but Cam could hear her moving about inside.

"Ahoy, Captain, permission to come aboard?"

Squirt's head popped up at the sound of Cam's voice. "Permission granted," she called down to her sister.

Cam slowly climbed the steps to reach the treehouse, then entered to sit beside Squirt. She noticed the dried blood on her shirt and face from a bloodied nose but didn't comment. Instead, Cam reached into her hoodie and pulled out the cookies, handing two to Squirt. She bit into a cookie and moaned. "I swear these get better every time Mom makes them."

Squirt took a bite. "I think you may be right."

"You think? Of course, I'm right. I am the great Cam St. Angelo," Cam answered with a chuckle. "Do you want to talk about what happened at school today?" When Sandy looked up at Cam, she could see tear stains on her cheeks, and Cam's heart ached for her baby sister.

"It was that danged Riley LaRue's fault. He tried to kiss me when we were waiting for the bus to come home. I didn't want to kiss him, so I pushed him away, and he slugged me."

"That little brute," Cam growled. "Wait until I get my hands on him."

"You don't need to do anything," Squirt told her. "Riley won't be trying to kiss me again after the whooping I gave him."

"Did ya beat the brakes off him?" Cam smirked.

"He ended up with more than a bloody nose. He will have one heck of a shiner for a few days, and I think I loosened up a tooth." She lifted her right hand to show Cam.

Cam saw skin scraped from her knuckles after contact with Riley's teeth and face. "That looks painful."

"It did hurt for a little while, but Riley sat in front on the bus ride home. I think he got my message."

"I'd say so," Cam said as she ruffled Squirt's hair. "You know, though, that you can't always use your fists to settle an argument, right?"

"Yes, Cam. But he wouldn't take a no for an answer. Ms. Judith, the school bus driver, stopped me when I went to get off the bus."

"What did she say?"

"She whispered to me that the little shit had it coming, and winked as she opened the door for me to leave."

"That sounds like something Ms. Judith would say. She's seen many of us kids grow up in the years she's been driving that bus."

"She looks older than dirt."

"Hey now. Ms. Judith ain't that old. She's delivered your sisters and me home from school for years without fail." Cam popped the last bite of cookie in her mouth as she sat next to Squirt. The sun was beginning to set across the bayou, and the bellow of a bull gator broke the silence. "You know what? I think it's time for me to tell you the story of the day you were born."

"What story, Cam?"

"I was sitting out on the front porch the night you arrived. Our sisters had already gone to bed, but I was determined to wait up for Dad to come home." Cam paused to look down at Squirt to find she had her full attention. "I was nearly asleep when the truck's headlights lit up the driveway, and I snapped to attention. Dad sat down beside me when he arrived and wrapped his arm around my shoulders. He said that you had finally arrived, and you both were resting well." Cam took a deep breath. "Then he told me this story. You would be the last born into the family, and as the oldest, it was my responsibility to look after you and

4

help you on your path in life. As you grew older, it would be your choice with my guidance to follow in my footsteps or choose to make your own path in the world."

"So, I'm like a job for you?" Sandy squinted up at Cam, not fully understanding the story.

"I reckon some would see it like that. Not me. I see it as a great privilege to bond with someone I love so dearly and to help you along your way. I'd be honored if you follow in my footsteps, but even more proud if you choose to blaze a path no one else has taken." Cam could still see the confusion on Sandy's face. "Does that make sense?"

"I think so. I'm just proud to have the great Cam St. Angelo for a sister." Sandy bumped into Cam with her shoulder. "I'm just teasing, but I do love you and feel closer to you than my other sisters."

"We are destined to be a team. I wouldn't want it any other way." Cam slipped an arm around Sandy's shoulders. "Are you ready to head home, Squirt? We need to get you cleaned up and that shirt soaking before that blood sets in permanently. You know, I think Mom is cooking pork chops for supper."

"That sounds good. I'm hungry."

"You know what else?" Cam asked as she stood and pulled Sandy to her feet. "My love for you grows with each passing day. I couldn't have asked for a better partner to share this world. I hope the world is ready for the two of us."

CHAPTER ONE

Months after Camille's death, Cam and Ronny sat down to discuss her future and the family businesses. Cam had done a fantastic job of helping him raise her four sisters while keeping the income steady. They had created Gator Girlz, Inc. to incorporate several of their business ventures and provide a future business structure. Ronny understood that Cam was wholly committed to her family, but he also knew she had a dream cut short by her mother's death. When Cam approached him about returning for a final year at LSU, Ronny eagerly agreed to her request. Teresa had just graduated from high school, and even though she and Buster would soon be married, they would continue to live on the homestead. He could rely on T to help him out during the day in Cam's absence, and her soon-to-be husband, Buster, could be counted on to help during the intense but short gator season. The price for harvested gators was looking high this year, so he would be well rewarded for filling his allotted tags. Cam would be home as often as she could during the gator season to help, and running a second boat would help them end their season sooner. He had managed the family business for years, so he felt confident they could survive nine months without Cam there to help him. Life without Camille was difficult for all of them, and Cam had sacrificed so much for the family. Ronny couldn't deny her request for a final year at college. The oldest of the five girls, Cam never had an opportunity to enjoy her childhood, and even though she loved her life on the bayou, he knew she hungered for more.

†

Cam was excited when her dad agreed that another year of college would help her and the business. She was excited to get the opportunity to have one more season of college softball and another year with Tab to discover what, if any, future they had together. Tab would be graduating and relocating to North Carolina to attend law school, so their time together would more than likely end when she graduated. Cam knew that Tab loved her, but as with her family, Tab's family had certain expectations for her future, which included law school and passing the bar exam. There was little room for a long-distance relationship for either of them in the future, so they were determined to enjoy the time they had together.

Cam's classes focused on business administration to add knowledge and skills that would help her run Gator Girlz, Inc. Coach was delighted she had returned for another shot at Oklahoma City, the host site for the College Softball World

Series and knew that Cam would be instrumental in motivating her team to get to the tournament. With Ruth, and now Liz, graduated, it was in the hands of Cam, Tab, and Parker to lead the team. Bugsy was, well, she was still Bugsy. Even though Cam had made it abundantly clear she had no interest in her, Bugsy continued to carry a simmering desire for Cam. After their altercation during their freshman year that nearly got Bugsy bounced from the team, she had at least learned not to make physical advances to Cam. It didn't keep her from shooting verbal cracks at Cam whenever she could, but Cam had grown adept at ignoring Bugsy's crude remarks.

Cam worked hard to make the most of the opportunity. She carried more classes than she had intended and took full advantage of her final year. Cam dedicated the fall semester to get in the best shape possible, and the coach had been right when Cam picked up a bat; that sweet swing was still there. With her improved physical conditioning, her power had also grown. Coach grinned from ear to ear when she watched balls sailing across the fence in all areas of the field. The team was more potent than it had been in many years, and Cam was determined to lead them to OKC.

Her relationship with Tab continued to thrive, and when she went home with her over a long weekend break, Tab's mother appeared to have warmed up to her. As much as she thought she could. Cam knew Tab's mother was a social snob and would always see her as just a poor Cajun kid from the bayou, but Cam survived the weekend unscathed. Tab's father, still a joy to be around, sent his wife off on a shopping adventure which gave him time to spend with Cam and his daughter. They had a great time cooking steaks and drinking beer on the spacious deck around the pool.

Later, when they were kissing to say goodnight before they departed for separate bedrooms, Cam turned to Tab. "I wish we could always have days like this. I've had a great time this weekend." She could see the pained look on Tab's face. They both knew their time together was coming to an end.

"It was great to be together here even for a few short days. Thank you for coming with me. I know mother doesn't always make it pleasant for you."

"She has a very high standard for you, and I fully understand she wants only the best for her daughter."

"What she will never understand is that you are the best for me. I've never been as happy as I've been with you."

Cam saw tears pooling in her eyes. "You can't say we haven't had some fun times."

"I've learned so much from you and your family that I'd never have learned anywhere else. To have the love your family shares is almost magical and without Sandy I'd probably never have learned I love to fish."

"That kid certainly loves fishing with you."

"I'll never forget the good times we have shared there. Even if I was the butt of more than one joke." Tab smiled and pulled Cam into a hug. "Let's plan to leave early tomorrow. I need to be naked in your arms."

"Is it tomorrow yet?" Cam grinned.

"No, but it will be soon. Goodnight, my love."

"Goodnight, Tab. Love you."

"More," Tab answered, and stepped inside her room.

Cam smiled at her answer, the same response she got from Sandy and the rest of her family. She turned and walked into the guest room. Tab did love her, and knowing that would not make it any easier for them to walk away from one another at the end of the year.

†

During the ride back to school the following day, Cam received a call from Sandy. "Hey, Squirt. What's up?" Cam listened to Sandy's excited chatter for several minutes. "Of course, I'll be there. Yes, I'll ask Tab if she wants to go and let you know this week. Okay, love to everyone for me. See you soon." She chuckled when she ended the call.

"Sandy and Wanda are both playing basketball in a holiday tournament, and they want us to come and watch."

"When it is?"

"The weekend we get out for the semester. Two weeks before Christmas."

"You do realize that's only a week away. I hope you'll tell Sandy we'll both come." Tab answered with a smile.

"They will both love that. Dad says it seems like forever since you've visited."

"Well, we haven't spent much time there this semester. I only got to join you for one weekend during the gator season in October. That weekend went by much too fast."

"Maybe you can spend a few extra days with us before you go home for Christmas."

"I'd really like that."

"This is going to be a tough one. Our first without Mama."

"She'll be smiling down on you all. I can guarantee that." Tab reached over and squeezed Cam's hand.

"Yes, she will." Cam turned her face to the window to hide the tears that were welling in her eyes. She knew the entire family felt Camille's absence, and she would do her best to make it a good holiday for them all. Cam had been spending time Christmas shopping and would cook all of her mama's holiday dishes with her sister's help. When she had been home for Thanksgiving, Sandy had already pulled out the Nativity Scene Camille had given them last year and positioned it on the mantel. The family had agreed on a fresh tree. Wanda and Sandy were eager for the assignment to find the tree for the family. A smile came to her face as Cam visualized Sandy and Wanda driving the Gator across the island in search of the perfect tree. She hoped that Buster and Jeff had done some culling, and there would be a pig roasting for a pig pickin during the holidays. The smell of roasting meat was always present during a St. Angelo holiday. Cam was confident more would be cooked to provide food for families in the area who didn't have the means for a holiday feast without the St. Angelo family's generosity. It had become a tradition years ago; one she was sure they would carry on for generations to come. She looked back at Tab. "Time for a pig pickin."

"That's always a great time around the St. Angelo home place. Will it be before or after Christmas? I'd love to be there."

"We will probably hold off until New Year's so everyone can start the year off with a full stomach."

"I can definitely make that. Mom and Dad are going on their annual cruise."

Cam chuckled. "How much longer do you think your dad's going to withstand that torture?"

"He hates them, but he does it for her. Love makes you do things you don't care for sometimes. At least in our family, it does."

"I can't say that it's ever happened in ours. We all love to celebrate together."

"You have the perfect family. Nobody ever seems cross or angry about anything." Tab sighed. "Maybe one day mine will be like that."

Cam reached over to cover Tab's hand with hers. "I'll do everything in my power to make it a great holiday for you."

"You always make me happy. Always, never forget that."

Cam simply nodded as they crossed the bridge into Baton Rouge. "Home sweet home."

CHAPTER TWO

Cam's final year at LSU ended all too soon. The softball season had gone well, and the team won the SEC tournament with Cam's walk-off home run in the seventh inning. The team's excellent play enabled them to host regional and super-regional games before making the World Series cut in OKC. Tab would miss graduation, but she preferred to join her team at the tournament. When they reached OKC and walked onto the field for their first practice, Tab smiled at Cam.

"We finally made it."

"Yes, we did." Cam's dream of playing in the national tournament was about to become a reality. It was worth all the sacrifice and hard work to stand on the infield of hallowed ground finally. She bent down and picked up a handful of the infield clay and let it sift through her fingers. The team would play three games before being eliminated from the tournament, but Cam would cherish those final hours playing the game she loved.

They made it back to Louisiana just in time to make Wanda's high school graduation. The coach was disappointed Wanda didn't have any interest in playing softball. Wanda preferred to study hard and graduate early to return to the bayou.

†

Tab spent a final three weeks on the island with Cam. She would be moving to North Carolina soon to start law school. Parker, one of their teammates, had landed a graduate assistant position at Duke, and at least Tab would have a friend at her new school. She and Parker would be living at the same apartment complex, so they would often see each other. Cam had mixed feelings about the latest development when she heard the news. She was jealous of Parker for remaining close to Tab but also glad that Tab wouldn't be alone. *You can't have it both ways.* They both understood that when Tab left Cam's home in Morganza, their relationship would be over. Life was too short for them to attempt a long-distance relationship, and they would have to settle for the few short years they had shared. Cam would always look back on them as some of the best of her life.

When their final night together came, Cam cooked steaks for them, and they shared a night of slow lovemaking. When they had snuggled in for the night, Cam wrapped her arm around Tab's shoulder. "Thank you for teaching me how to love."

"You already knew how to do that quite well," Tab reminded her.

"You know what I mean."

"There's so much you and your family have taught me. I think it was a fair trade." She chuckled, making Cam smile in the dark.

Cam cleared her throat. "I hope you will find another love like ours."

"Right now, all I want is to finish school. There will never be another you in my life. What we have is special, and I hope we can remain friends and you will find a forever love."

"I will always be right here if you find your way back."

"And you will always be right here," Tab said, took Cam's hand, and laid it above her heart.

Cam felt the tears slide down her cheeks. Life had tossed them another curveball; one she wouldn't be able to attack emotionally. She could only hope working with her family would help fill the gaping hole of Tab's absence. They both knew this day would come, but Cam couldn't comprehend how difficult saying goodbye to Tab would be.

The next morning, after a final breakfast with the family, Cam walked out with Tab to her car. "I miss you already," she said as she slipped Tab's bag in the trunk. She wrapped Tab in her arms for a final hug. "Let me know you've made it home."

"I will," Tab answered as her tears began to fall. "I will always love you, Cam."

"I know, and I feel the same, but we just aren't meant to be." She opened the door for Tab and closed it behind her. "Stay safe and keep in touch."

Tab simply nodded and started the engine. She looked up at Cam one final time and then pulled slowly away.

Cam watched her disappear and then walked to the dock to take her boat back to the island.

†

Sandy and Wanda had watched the exchange from the living room window. When they saw Cam walk past the house, they started for the back door to follow her.

"You two stay here," Ronny called from the kitchen. "Cam needs some time alone right now. Let's give her some space."

Wanda groaned, knowing that Tab's heart would be breaking. She remembered how she felt when Logan, her first love, moved away after their short relationship. Wanda felt like her heart had been ripped from her chest. Even though they hadn't been together nearly as long as Tab and Cam, she remembered the intense pain.

"Why can't Cam go with her?" Sandy had asked.

"Some things are just not meant to be *ma cherie*," Ronny had told her. "Some people come into our lives for specific reasons and for just a limited time."

"Like Tab?" she asked.

"Yes, like Tab, but now it's time for her to move on to follow her dreams."

"That just doesn't seem right," Sandy said. "They love each other so much."

"Sometimes love doesn't fit in with what life has in store for us, but there will be others ahead for the both of them."

Sandy listened to her dad's wise words. Even though she didn't understand them completely, she trusted his answer.

†

Sandy had finally hit a growth spurt and was excelling at two sports, basketball and softball. Her senior year in high school brought a new softball coach to the high school, a fresh graduate from Ole Miss, with experience playing on the Division One level.

Sandy and the new coach, Lisa, had grown close during the season and the team won the state title for the first time since Cam graduated. However, as it goes all too often, Lisa was offered an assistant coach position at Ole Miss and the blossoming friendship came to a screeching halt. Lisa did provide encouragement to Sandy when she talked about her teammate, Missy, but after a few dates, Sandy knew Missy wasn't the one. Missy moved away that summer to start college, something Sandy had absolutely no interest in doing. Sandy occasionally thought of the first night she had spent with Missy out on the island. It was a week after graduation and Missy had spent the day with Sandy out on the bayou fishing. Missy had talked nonstop about how excited she was to be going off to college and playing ball at Ole Miss with their former coach, Lisa. Sandy listened intently for the first hour, then tuned her out to concentrate on fishing.

After dropping the catch off at JB's for processing, Sandy drove them to the island. They used one of the Gators to tour and Sandy pointed out several young fawns grazing in a marshy meadow. Cam had taken the night off from cooking shine to give them privacy on the island. Sandy built a campfire and cooked steaks for dinner. Missy had spotted some beer in the refrigerator and the two teens had a good buzz by the time the fire died down. When they called it a night, Sandy stripped down and was showering when a draft from the door opening alerted her to Missy's presence. Missy stepped into the shower and turned Sandy to face her.

Their first deep kiss was shared in that shower and they spent several hours that night learning how to make love. The first time felt awkward, but once Sandy allowed her body to relax and enjoy the pleasure, the sensations rushed through her. Something was missing, however, and the next day, Sandy realized what it was. She and Missy had a deep friendship, but they weren't in love. Their night of passion was just that, experimentation for two fledgling lesbians with no emotional connection. Sandy knew enough from watching her older siblings that true love was much different than what she felt for Missy.

When Missy left for college, Sandy was disappointed; however, she wasn't invested in the relationship enough to feel the devastating heartbreak of losing a first crush. She would always appreciate Missy for being her first lover, but her heart belonged in the bayou with the family. Had Missy even attempted to plea for Sandy to join her in Oxford, where she would be playing ball for Lisa, Sandy would have turned her down. The bayou nourished her soul with its beautiful landscapes, hardworking and deeply loving people, and Sandy knew this is where she belonged. With Cam back at home, the Gator Girlz business was thriving, and Sandy would continue to be a pulse in the company's heart.

Sandy had experienced the tug at her heartstrings with Missy, but she was content spending her days and nights with Cam as they worked together to continue building the family business. She and Cam had become inseparable since she graduated from high school. There was rarely a time when you saw one that the other was far away. Sandy had become an expert at driving the airboat and would accompany Cam on night deliveries of the moonshine. On more than a few occasions, Sandy's skills at the controls had

18

kept them from being tracked down by Fish and Game authorities as they patrolled the bayou for bootleggers. When a new deputy came to town and caught Cam's attention, Sandy was jealous at first. Then she realized Cam was ready to move on from Tab and open her heart to the possibility of love. Since their dad, Ronny, had died three years after losing Camille, the family business success weighed heavily on Cam's shoulders. If anyone deserved to have a new love in her life, it was indeed Cam.

CHAPTER THREE

Sandy walked into the house to find Cam standing in the middle of the living room, her eyes glued to the weather channel. She shrugged off her dripping wet coat and hung it by the door. "Will this rain ever end?"

Cam jumped when she heard Sandy's voice. "Damn, I didn't hear you come in."

"Sorry. I didn't mean to startle you. What's the forecast?"

Cam ran a hand through her hair, a sure sign of her distress for the people trying to escape the rapidly rising floodwaters. "More damned rain. There's no sign of it letting up anytime soon. Already nearing twenty inches."

"I don't know anywhere that can handle that amount of rain in such a short period without flooding. Especially in towns surrounded by rivers and streams. Where are they broadcasting from?"

Cam turned her head back to the television. "Livingston and Tangipahoa Parish. Livingston seems to be getting the worst of it right now." She turned to look at Sandy. "The Amite, Comite, and Tangipahoa rivers have swelled beyond anything ever recorded."

"So many lives ruined." Sandy sighed deeply. "Is there anything we can do to help? Not much we can do here with all this damned rain."

"I've been mulling that over all day. I think it's time for this family to join the Cajun Navy and help out our neighbors in need."

"Yes!" Sandy hollered. "I'd love to do that. We can take my airboat. It'll maneuver better in the floodwaters and is faster than anything else we have."

"That does sound wise. Get on the phone and call the sisters together for a meeting after supper."

"I'm all over it, Cam." Sandy sprinted into the kitchen.

Cam continued to watch the coverage as she began to form a plan. She and Sandy could head south for a few days, and the rest of the family could keep the homestead safe. The rain was relatively light in the area, especially compared to Baton Rouge. She was glad she had heeded her dad's advice to elevate her home on pylons when she chose to build so near to the water. Four feet off the ground should be safe from anything short of a catastrophic event.

"All set," Sandy called from the kitchen as she opened up the refrigerator. "You really need to do some grocery shopping, Cam." She opened up a drawer and pulled out some sliced cheese.

Cam laughed, "It just hasn't been a big priority. I can always go play pitiful and get a hot meal from T, Wanda, or Karen if I get desperate."

Sandy dropped the cheese on the counter. "How old is that bread?"

"Probably the newest purchase in the house. You gonna make us some grilled cheese sandwiches?"

"I was thinking about it. Otherwise, it's pretty slim pickin's in here." She opened a cabinet and pulled out a frying pan. "Knowing you, you're already making a list in your head of supplies we need. Go ahead and sit at the table and start writing. I'll have sandwiches up in no time." She shuffled through the pantry. "At least tell me you have some sweet pickles."

"In the fridge, bottom door shelf."

Cam settled in at her small kitchen table and started compiling the list of supplies they would take with them.

"So, how's it going with that sexy new deputy?"

"We've been out a few times, to dinner mostly. I think once we get back, it may be time to step things up a notch."

"You could definitely do with a woman's touch around here, Cam," Sandy replied as she searched through cabinets to find plates.

"I'm not sure Luce is any more housewife material than I am."

"You're doomed then." Sandy feigned a look of despair.

"I don't see you dating anyone, so don't complain."

"Hey, I'm still young and single. I'm not getting long in the tooth." Sandy couldn't help but laugh at her witty comment.

"I may be older, but I can still put a whooping on your ass, baby sister."

"I do not doubt that at all, but someone like Luce won't stay single for long. It's not like we have a plethora of eligible females available in our little slice of heaven."

"That's very true, and I will make it a point to address Luce when I return."

Sandy turned on the burner to cook. "Are you planning to tell her you're going out of town for a few days at least?"

"Honestly, I hadn't given it any thought, but now that we are planning to go, I think it might be a good idea. I'll shoot Luce a text and see if she's available for dinner."

"You'll have to take her out somewhere. You sure don't have anything to cook here." Sandy broke out laughing.

"I don't live with Liz and Wanda and have a serious home-cooked meal to come home to every day," Cam shot back at her. She picked up her phone and sent a text to Luce.

When she returned to her list, she looked up at Sandy. "Do you need any supplies? I'm low on ammo, so I thought I'd make a run to town."

Sandy flipped a sandwich. "I think we could both use a new set of Frogg Toggs to help keep us dry."

"That's a great idea. Extra small for you?" Cam teased.

"A men's small fits me well," Sandy replied. "I've graduated from kid sizes."

Cam's phone pinged with a text, bringing a smile to Cam's face. "Luce is off at six. That will give me time to shop, have a nice dinner, and get home before it gets late. I'd like to have an early start tomorrow. Can you handle informing the others of our plans?"

"Yeah, no problem. I'll get my gear packed up, too, so we'll be all set for in the morning. I'll make a fuel run as well."

A bolt of lightning flashed across the bayou, illuminating the windows.

"That was close," Cam said as Sandy brought over a stack of sandwiches. "I hope that passes through tonight. I don't cherish being in a metal boat with lightning striking the area." Sandy turned toward the kitchen. "Please tell me you have something to drink."

"A couple of sodas are hiding behind the milk."

Sandy picked up the plastic carton and shook the contents. "Is that what you call this? Cam, it expired over two weeks ago." She plucked out two bottles of soda. "Do I need to start grocery shopping for you?"

"No, I'll start giving Karen a list that she can add when she goes shopping. I'm sure she wouldn't mind picking up some extra items."

"You need to start eating better." Sandy slipped into a seat beside her. "We can't have you shriveling up and blowing away on us."

Cam took a bite of the sandwich. "Won't have to worry as long as you make me grilled cheese."

"You cannot survive on those alone. I'll come and cook for you if I need to."

"It's usually so late by the time we drag in the last thing I think about is cooking."

Sandy nodded. "We could always cook some things to toss in the freezer so that all you would need was to warm them up."

"Are you that worried about me?" Cam asked.

"You've been losing weight lately. I can't have you getting sick on me." Sandy smiled at her. "We've lost too much already."

Cam nodded. With their parents' deaths and Tab going off to law school, she did feel a deep sense of loss. "I'll do better."

"Great. So, let's take a look at the list you've made." Sandy reached across for the notepad and added a few items.

"Looks like we have most of this on hand. I'll pack the supplies and have them ready to load into the back of your truck unless you want to take the Jeep."

"We have more storage space in the truck. Easier to sleep in, too, if necessary."

"I hadn't thought of that. Should we pack some sleeping bags, an air mattress, and pillows just in case?"

"That may not be a bad idea. Camping on the ground is out of the question, but the truck sleeps fairly comfortable." Cam looked at Sandy. "You realize we may see some horrible things down there, right? We may run across dead bodies that can look pretty gruesome."

Sandy sighed. "I hope we can get there in time to prevent some of that from happening."

"Me, too, but you have to prepare for the eventuality. Nothing I want to see, but it's possible."

Sandy glanced up at the television. "There are some hard-hit areas. I just hope we can do some good."

"We won't know until we try. Eat up. I'm going to throw some clothes together in a suitcase. Thanks for making me eat."

"Thanks for eating. I know we all miss Mama's cooking, but it will soon be time to start having some boils, cookouts, and pig pickins. We will all eat well then."

"Tru dat," Cam answered. "If it's not too late when I get home, we can go ahead and load the truck and hook up the airboat."

"Or you can take my Jeep, and I'll load the truck while you're gone."

"That's a great idea. I haven't driven the old gal for a while."

"Just be kind to her," Sandy replied. "She may be old, but she's reliable."

"I'll clean up the kitchen and see you in a bit then," Cam said as Sandy headed for the door.

"Deal. I'm going to pack my bag and bring it over." Sandy turned and looked at Cam. "We're doing a good thing, right?"

"Yeah, we are. I think we can do some good for our community."

"Have fun and tell Luce I said hello. Take her someplace for a nice meal."

Cam nodded. "We're going for a steak dinner."

"That's an excellent plan. See ya."

†

Cam finished the kitchen clean up, and walked to her bedroom. It had been some time since she had traveled anywhere, so she had to remember where she stored her small suitcase. She found it in the laundry room closet and dusted it off. Cam tossed in several pairs of jeans, long sleeve shirts, socks, and underwear. If they were gone longer, they could find a laundromat if needed. She added a pair of camp shoes to allow her boots some time to air out and her hygiene kit. She had no idea if they would have an opportunity for hot showers or meals. Cam decided they would take some snacks and fresh water. If she couldn't take a shower, she could at least brush her teeth. After packing, Cam carried her bag to the front door. She picked up her list and walked over to find Sandy to retrieve the Jeep keys.

†

Sandy and Wanda were in the kitchen when Cam walked in. "It smells like cookies in here," she said.
"Wanda is making cookies and brownies for us to take." Sandy smiled at her older sisters.

"I thought I'd pick up some jerky and other easy snacks too. I don't know what the food or lodging situation will be like farther south. Any special requests?"

"Sunflower seeds," Sandy replied. "The ones with the shells on."

"That's easy enough. Anything else?"

"Some peanut butter crackers and sleeves of peanuts. A case of Mountain Dew for some caffeine. I'll pull out a cooler."

"All right then. I'm gone. See you soon."

Wanda looked up from the cookies. "Say hiya to Luce and invite her out for dinner when y'all get back home. I'll make a big pan of lasagna or something."

Cam chuckled. "Will do. Your lasagna will be incentive enough to get her out here."

†

The rain had finally let up when Cam drove to town. The air smelled fresh, with everything washed clean by the recent deluge. Critters were on the move, too, with the break in the rain. Frogs leaped across the paved road, and Cam witnessed a mama cat carrying a kitten, presumably to higher ground. Everyone and everything had to work hard at surviving in the bayou. There were no exceptions. Cam pulled into a local outdoor shop and scanned her list for the needed items. She could spend all day in the store browsing the aisles of outdoor equipment, but Cam remained disciplined and followed her list of required items. The only thing Cam added were several coils of rope. They hadn't been on her original plan, but she felt like there would be a need for it on their adventure. Cam loaded her purchases in the back seat of the Jeep and drove to her next stop. The grilled cheese sandwich Squirt had made her was long gone, and Cam's stomach began rumbling as she selected snacks for their trip. She still thought of her young sister more as Squirt than Sandy. Looking at the half-filled cart brought a smile to her face. Cam had probably purchased an excessive amount for their journey, but what they didn't consume, she would use to fill her empty pantry. That might show Squirt her commitment to eating better, or at least more often. Her concern for Cam had warmed her heart. Cam couldn't be prouder of the young woman Squirt was becoming. She would always have a wild and reckless spirit, but no one took work more seriously when it came to family or business.

Cam glanced at her watch and saw she was running close on time. She returned the cart and jogged back to the Jeep. When Cam pulled out of the lot headed for the restaurant to meet Luce, she saw a sheriff's cruiser sitting in an empty parking lot across the street. Mirrored aviator glasses watched her approach, and Cam nodded to Bugsy as she passed. Bugsy, a teammate of Cam's in college, had long carried a torch for her even after her foolish attempts nearly got her removed from the softball team. Cam was surprised when Bugsy took a job in the local law enforcement agency. Still, so far, she had only been a minor nuisance. Bugsy would occasionally pull Cam or Sandy over just as a reminder that she was in the area and watching Cam close for illegal activities. Bugsy was right on one account, but Cam had been able to outwit Bugsy up to this point. Bugsy seemed to sense that Cam and her family made moonshine, but she could prove little without proper evidence. Cam was careful not to allow her to find that. Cam also worried that once word got out that she was dating Luce, a fellow officer, Bugsy's harassment might worsen. If and when it did, Cam would play her ace in the hole. One of her top customers just so happened to be the sheriff. Cam let out a soft chuckle as she shifted gears and rolled into the parking lot at the same time Luce arrived.

Luce stepped out of her car, still dressed in her uniform. Cam felt her breath hitch every time Luce smiled at her. She parked beside her and stepped out of the Jeep.

"That was perfect timing," Luce said. "Where's your truck?"

"At home. Sandy is packing it tonight."

"Are you going somewhere?" Luce asked as they walked to the door.

Cam nodded. "Let's get seated, and I'll fill you in on our plan."

Once they had placed food orders, Luce looked at Cam. "Okay, spill it. I'm curious about this mystery trip."

"Squirt and I have decided to join the Cajun Navy and go south to help rescue some of the residents stranded in this damn flood."

"Oh," Luce said, and sat back in her seat.

"We're heading out in the morning and will use the airboat to help any way we can," Cam continued.

"I've been watching the reports on the news and coming into the station. There is terrible devastation happening down there. It's a dangerous environment there right now with looters, pissed-off wildlife, and crumbling homes."

"I promise we will be careful," Cam replied.

"Not to be morose, but you'll more than likely run across deceased persons during your search. Victims of drowning can be especially gruesome sights. Are y'all prepared for that?"

Cam swallowed hard. "I'm not sure we could ever prepare for that, but I feel compelled to go help if we can."

"I wish I could go along. I've volunteered for some double shifts this week to make sure our community stays safe."

"That would have been nice, but I understand you're needed here. I just wanted to let you know if you don't hear from me for a few days, not to worry."

Luce smiled. "Thank you. You may not have much reception down there. I hope they will outfit you with radios to stay in communication with the rescue efforts."

"Sandy and I have a set for use out on the bayou. If we can tune into their channel, it shouldn't be a problem."

When the food arrived, Cam dove into the meal.

"You must have been hungry," Luce said with a twinkle in her eyes.

"Getting supplies and planning is hard work. Not like what we would be doing out on the bayou, but yeah, I worked up an appetite. Speaking of which, Sandy and Wanda said 'hello,' and Wanda wants you to come for dinner when we get back. She's offering up her legendary lasagna if you'll come."

"Please tell her I'd really like that. I'm looking forward to seeing the St. Angelo compound and meeting the rest of your family."

Cam smiled. "Hopefully, that won't scare you off."

Luce reached over and covered Cam's hand. "I don't scare easily."

"That's a good thing." Cam enjoyed a lingering touch from Luce until the waitress returned to the table to refill their drinks.

"Maybe if I'm off that day, you can give me the tour of the bayou. I haven't seen much of it since I arrived," Luce suggested.

"You shall have the grand tour then," Cam answered.

"How long do you think you will be gone?"

"I don't imagine more than three to four days. After that, I think the mission will shift to recovery instead of rescues. We won't be of use for that and will come home."

Luce smiled at Cam. "I'm proud of the two of y'all for helping out."

"It feels like the right thing to do, and we've got weeks left to prepare for gator season."

"Ah, I forget the Gator Girlz are renowned gator hunters. Maybe I can go out with you one day for some experience."

"It's hard work, but we will always welcome an extra set of hands."

"It's a thirty-day season, right?"

"Unless it's cut short by weather or some other event. The prices are forecast to be good this year, so we're hopeful of a good season. I've upped our tags for this year to three hundred and fifty."

Luce let out a low whistle. "That's a lot of gators to catch in thirty days."

"We run two boats now, so I'm confident we can fill them all. I'd hate to waste hard-earned money on tags we don't use."

"Ouch. I bet that could be costly," Luce replied.

"It also drops the number we can apply for next year. So, for those thirty days, we will be busting it from sunrise to sunset."

"That sounds like a lot of hard work. Very impressive, Ms. St. Angelo."

"Why, thank you, officer. I always aim to finish the job."

Luce chuckled. "I'm sure you do."

The waitress approached and asked them about dessert.

"There's no way I can eat anything else." Cam groaned.

"You certainly did a number on that steak, Cam," the waitress teased. She pulled the bill from her apron. Luce moved quickly to pick it up and handed the woman a credit card.

"I intended to pay since I asked you out," Cam told Luce.

"It was my turn, and I want you to know how proud of you I am. Do I need to start saluting you and calling you Captain St. Angelo?"

Cam chuckled and shook her head. "No, that would be Sandy. We're taking her airboat, and she's a much better driver than I am."

As they walked to their vehicles, Cam spoke softly. "I'll try to give you a call, but don't worry if you don't hear from me."

"Just promise me you'll be careful and take care of yourselves."

"I promise. I'll let you know when we're heading back. Thanks for the lovely dinner." Cam pulled Luce into a hug. "I'll see you soon."

"Goodnight, Cam. Get some rest."

"I will." Cam waited until Luce got in her cruiser and pulled away. Her eyes followed Luce until she turned right headed for home, and Cam spotted Bugsy across the street.

"Fucking stalker," Cam growled and climbed into the Jeep. She drove past Bugsy without even a glance as she made her way home.

†

"All set? Wanda asked Sandy as she brought another bag to the front porch.

"All I need to do is toss the bags into the back of the truck. I've already gotten the rest of the supplies loaded, and the airboat fueled and hooked up to the trailer hitch."

Wanda pointed to a large basket. "I've put cookies, brownies, and a fresh loaf of bread in with a jar of peanut butter and jelly. There's a new batch of egg salad you can place in the cooler with your drinks for lunch tomorrow. Before you ask, yes, there's a jar of sweet pickles too."

"Sounds like we're all set. Thank you for everything."

"I'm very proud of the two of y'all for helping out. You represent our family and community well."

"Romeo should be home soon, and I can pack the rest of the goodies and hit the sack. I'm not sure I'll get much sleep, though."

"You need to try. It may be the last decent night's sleep you get for a while," Wanda reminded her. "Did you think to pack solar chargers and headlamps?"

Sandy nodded. "Already in the airboat console."

"Are y'all packing protection?" Liz asked from the kitchen.

"Yes, ma'am. I've got my magnum, and Cam's taking her nine."

"That should knock down anything you run across," Liz chuckled.

Sandy nodded. "I pray we won't need them, but better to be prepared than to be caught off guard."

Wanda cocked her head at Sandy. "Where did my wild buck of a little sister go? You sound all grown up all of a sudden."

Liz hugged her wife. "If you haven't noticed lately, that little girl has grown into an adorable young woman."

Sandy's face blushed profusely.

"Do I need to be worried?" Wanda asked Liz.

"No, baby. I only have eyes for you, but you have to admit she's as cute as a button."

"Okay, you two can stop now," Sandy said, flustered by Liz's compliment.

"I bet there's a nurse or three at the hospital that would love a date with you," Liz said.

"No offense, ladies, but I'm not ready to settle down yet."

"Last time I checked the lesbian dating manual, you have to go on at least three dates before you order a U-Haul," Wanda teased. "We love you and want to see you having some fun and not working all the time."

"I don't—" Sandy started, but Liz cut her off.

"You won't win that argument, so leave it be. A date every blue moon wouldn't hurt."

"Yes, Mama," Sandy answered, and ducked away from the potholder Wanda threw at her. "Girl, you've lost the arm you had in high school. You used to be able to throw." Sandy giggled and headed for the door.

"I knew I should have laced those brownies with Ex-lax," Wanda said. "She may be the baby, but she's still full of shit."

"But you love her," Liz reminded her.

"Yes, I do."

"I love y'all too. I'll be back in a bit." Sandy grabbed the bag and went out the front door.

†

When Cam returned, it only took half an hour to finish packing. "I'll see you bright and early," Cam said when Sandy headed home for the night. "Rest up. We've got quite an adventure ahead of us."

"I'll be ready," Sandy answered. "Goodnight, Cam."

"Night, Squirt. Love ya."

"Most," Sandy answered and walked home.

†

Cam showered and dressed for bed. She picked up her phone and sent Luce a text.

Thanks again for dinner. See you soon.

My pleasure. Tell Wanda I'm looking forward to lasagna. Goodnight, and stay safe.

Goodnight, Luce.

Cam pulled the covers over her body and listened to the night sounds of the bayou. The rain had ended, and the chorus of night creatures lulled her to sleep.

CHAPTER FOUR

Sandy had loaded the cooler in the back of the truck and returned to Cam's with a paper plate filled with sausage biscuits. "Wanda's gift for the road," Sandy said as she took a bite.

"You gotta love that woman," Cam said and grabbed a biscuit. "Last bag, and I'm ready to go."

As they walked to the truck, the front door opened, and Wanda and Liz walked out. Liz was on her way to the hospital to start an early shift.

"You two come back safe," Liz said as she reached her car.

"Will do. Thanks for breakfast," Cam told Wanda.

"My pleasure. Call when you can." Wanda kissed Liz and then watched her sisters and wife drive away as the sun began to creep above the horizon.

Cam waited for Liz to pull ahead of them in the driveway then turned to Sandy. "Hand me another one of those biscuits, please."

Sandy passed her a meat-filled biscuit. "I don't know how she makes these taste so good."

"She learned how to put the love in them from Mama," Cam said.

"Maybe we should have paid more attention in the kitchen," Sandy said, then broke out in laughter. "Naw, we're not the kitchen type."

"Hey, speak for yourself. I can get quite creative in the kitchen when I put my mind to it," Cam corrected her.

"Hmm, I can remember a meal or two that didn't end up burnt," Sandy joked.

"You survived, didn't you?"

"Yeah, it could have been what stunted my growth, though." She laughed.

Cam smiled at her sister. "Well, you know what they say. The runt of the litter is always the best pick."

"That's for sure," Sandy said. "If you need a break from driving, let me know."

"As empty as the roads seem, we will be there much faster than usual."

"Where are we heading anyhow?" Sandy asked.

"You are just now wondering that?" Cam chuckled. "There's a command center set up near Denham Springs. I figured we'd start there."

Sandy stared out the window at the high water. In places, it lapped at the base of the bridges. "Have you ever seen flooding like this?"

Cam shook her head. "People say a flood like this only happens about every hundred years. If it's bad this far north, I can't imagine what it looks like down south."

"We will know that answer soon enough," Sandy replied.

†

When they reached Baton Rouge's outskirts, traffic slowed to a crawl as they approached the Interstate Ten Bridge crossing the Mississippi River. Trucks that typically traveled this route would be detoured off the main highways due to road closures. Relief supply vehicles moved slowly in the traffic jam. They would carry clean water and food supplies to the victims of the floods. Sandy noticed a string of trucks towing boats of varying sizes with banners emblazoned with *Cajun Navy*.

"It looks like we're in good company," Sandy said as she nodded toward the string of boats.

"Yeah, it does. Damn, would you look at that?" Cam pointed to the large football stadium known as Death Valley. "There appears to be several feet of water inside the stadium."

"The surrounding campus looks pretty waterlogged, too," Sandy said.

"The Big Muddy must have been pretty swollen too to dump that amount of water onto the University. She still looks pretty high. You should normally see loading docks there." Cam pointed out an area to Sandy.

"Not today," Sandy answered.

"Nope, there definitely won't be any loading or unloading happening today. Damn, this is bad. The outlying areas are much lower than sea level."

As the traffic began to creep ahead, the large trucks diverted to free up multiple traffic lanes allowed the flow to increase. Cam carefully followed the line of boats, and when they exited on O'Neal Lane, she turned to follow them.

"They seem to know where they are going. Let's follow them and find out."

The line of trucks pulled into a large parking lot still covered in places with six inches or more of water. Interstate Twelve had been closed ahead due to the flooding. There were three large white tents assembled in the lot, and Cam parked as close as she could to one of them. "It's time to get wet." She turned the engine off, and stepped out of the truck to follow a crowd of primarily men into a tent.

There were several tables set up beneath the tent. Cam approached and introduced herself and Sandy to one of the workers. "We brought an airboat, and we'd like to offer our help."

A weary-looking man smiled up at her. "We'll take all the help we can get. Have you ever done search and rescue before?"

"No, we haven't," Cam answered.

"That's not a problem. You will need to register and attend a short instructional course before we can give you an assignment. It takes less than an hour to complete." He nodded toward another older man. "This is Woody. He'll get you set up in the course and make sure you have everything you need. We don't have much in the way of accommodations, but there will be a hot meal waiting for you at the end of the day. Most of the hotels have received significant flood damage, but we do have access to hot showers at a local gym."

"We are prepared to sack out in our truck," Sandy said as they followed Woody to a small row of folding chairs.

"Hang tight, and we'll get started in just a few minutes."

Sandy and Cam took seats and were glad the rain had stopped, and they could open the walls of the tent to allow the slight breeze to flow through. It was midmorning, but the humidity hung like a curtain in the moist air.

A few minutes later, Woody returned with another small group of men and a uniformed man he introduced as Major Tom Walker of the National Guard. The two men sat amidst the small group and began to issue instructions on the search and rescue campaign methods. Sandy and Cam paid close attention to the training and noted each of the instructions. Each team received a box of neon spray paints to denote buildings they had checked for survivors. Each box had a laminated sheet with codes they would paint on the front door of each location. Major Walker went over these codes carefully.

"We must know which buildings have been searched, so our teams are not wasting time duplicating efforts. We estimate there may be at least a thousand citizens unaccounted for, and you will be assigned a heavily inhabited area to search."

Woody stood and handed each of the teams a laminated map and several grease pencils. "These are the locations and directions to the areas you will be searching. Check off each site with the pencil, and each night we can update our grids." He looked around the small group. "We've located and removed many casualties, but there will be more, so I want you to be prepared to find deceased individuals. We don't expect you to handle them, only note their location on your grids."

One of the men raised his hand. "What if the body is outside?"

"If you can safely move it into a sealed location, then do so. If the situation appears too dangerous, stay away and radio in the location. Do you all have radios?" Everyone in the group nodded. "We broadcast on channel fifteen, twelve, and seven."

A man looked nervously around the room. "Um, what do you mean by too dangerous?"

Woody took a deep breath. "Unfortunately, the floodwaters have brought gators, moccasins, and other nasty creatures into residential areas they would typically not enter. With the odor of death, these creatures may look for an easy meal. With their normal habitats affected also, they have become more aggressive."

Major Walker continued instruction. "When you pick up survivors, you will need to assess if they need immediate attention. If they do, bring them here as quickly and safely as possible. If they are in good shape, try to get several in your boats before returning to maximize our trips. If you run across a life-or-death situation, radio the location and remain onsite to assist with removal. We have helicopters available for immediate evacuation."

Woody cleared his throat. "The rains have stopped for now, and the floodwaters appear to be slowly receding, but we must remain diligent for what is heading our way from farther north. For those of you in airboats, you can launch from here with no problems. Heavier boats need to travel a mile or so down O'Neal for deeper water. I would recommend you leave your keys with me if we need to evacuate to a drier location."

"One final thing you will need." Major Walker handed each of the teams a *Cajun Navy* banner. "You should fly this at all times, so residents know you are there to help, not loot."

"Has that been a problem?" Sandy asked.

"Unfortunately, yes, in some areas. If you run across anyone that doesn't seem to belong at a site, do not intervene. If you can, take a picture of any vehicle and radio in the location, but do not interfere. A flood-damaged television is not worth any amount of harm. We don't expect you to work late into the night either. For your safety, we ask that you come in as close to dark-fall as you can. Hot meals will be available until ten o'clock, back here at this tent. Are there any questions?"

When no one answered, Woody stood up. "Thank you for volunteering, and be safe. If you want to leave your keys with me, just let me know."

Cam and Sandy left the tent and stowed the last of their gear on the airboat. They received a case of water for any survivors they ran across and for their own use. Cam pulled the truck off the edge of the highway into water that was a bit deeper, and they unloaded the boat. "I'm going to go park and give Woody the keys. I'll be right back if you want to start studying the map."

Sandy pulled out the *Cajun Navy* banner and hung it from a crossbeam.

Cam parked and pulled a small bag from the back seat before giving Woody the keys. She jogged back over to Sandy and pulled out a bright pink Gator Girlz ball cap. "I thought now would be a good time to start breaking these in."

"These are great. Thanks, Cam." Sandy adjusted her cap and placed it on her head. "All set?"

"Let's do this," Cam answered.

†

Sandy fired up the powerful engine. She carefully guided the boat through the shallow spots and then picked up speed once they hit deeper water. Cam sat beside Sandy as they worked their way farther into the devastated areas. Everywhere they looked, water almost entirely covered buildings in the area. Road signs that typically hung eight feet from the ground were barely visible, and they used the signs to follow their grid map. Once they passed the business section's remnants, apartments, hotels, and homes appeared, with severe damages.

"It looks like we have three miles to the Amite River where we will begin our search," Sandy shouted over the roar of the engine.

Sandy expertly guided the boat past floating cars and other flood debris as they remained vigilant for any signs of survivors along the route. The utter devastation of homes and businesses turned Sandy's stomach. There would be a significant loss for the economy along with the human casualties as many companies and jobs were lost. As they drew closer to the first homes marked on the grid, Sandy eased off the accelerator. They listened for any signs of movement or calls for help, but only an eerie silence covered the area. Just ahead on the left, Cam pointed out a small cinder block home, and Sandy eased up to the front porch.

Cam stepped off the boat, tied a rope to a front porch post, and then pulled a flashlight from her pocket. Cam turned back to Sandy.

"Stay here."

Sandy nodded. "Be careful."

Cam called out. "Is anyone home?" When there was no answer, she used her foot to push open the door. "Hello," she repeated as she stepped inside the home.

A foot of water remained inside the tiny house, but there was no sign of anyone anywhere. When she reached a small hallway, she saw a dropdown staircase that would lead into the attic. Cam carefully reached up and pulled the string to lower the stairs. She jumped backward when a box came tumbling toward her. Once her heart rate slowed, Cam shined her flashlight into the darkness.

"Is there anybody up there?"

Cam listened and heard a faint rustling. Slowly she ascended the steps until she could see the small attic space. Cam moved the beam of her flashlight around the area, finding it empty. She breathed a sigh of relief and backed down the stairs. After checking all rooms and doors for a second time, Cam was satisfied the house was vacant. She pulled the back door open with a tug and found a small barn. Unsure of the depth of the water, Cam decided to get back there on the airboat. She walked back through the house and untied the rope.

"Toss me the yellow can, please."

Sandy pulled out the bright yellow paint and tossed it over to Cam, who placed a yellow checkmark on the door. Sandy breathed a sigh of relief to see the symbol for empty. Cam stepped back onto the boat.

"There's a barn structure out back we need to check out."

Sandy nodded and started the engine. She quickly spun the boat in a circle and approached the barn. Ten feet away, the boat touched solid ground. "I think it's safe to step off here," she told Cam.

The barn door had blown open, and as Cam approached, she once more called out. "Is anyone here?" Cam searched the small building and left.

"Nothing," she told Sandy.

"On to the next?" Sandy asked.

Cam stepped onto the boat. "Yes, when you're ready."

They traveled several hundred yards farther down the trail before spotting a trailer that appeared to have previously sat on stilts. The water's power had knocked half of the trailer off the foundation, causing a break in the structure's roof. As they approached, the sisters were relieved to see the metal door push open, and an older woman climbed out onto the porch. Nestled in her arms was a small dog.

"Hello," Cam called out.

"I've never been so glad to see someone in my life. My name is Reba, and I've been praying for days for someone to come rescue me."

"We are Cam and Sandy," Cam said as she took the small dog and handed it to Sandy, and then helped Reba onto the airboat. "Is there anyone else inside?"

"No, it was just me until this little fellow came rushing by. He was lucky I had a fishnet on the porch and could snag him out of the fast-moving water. That was two days ago."

"Are you hurt anywhere?" Sandy asked.

"No, I was fortunate to be in the front half of the trailer when the water broke through. It was in the middle of the night and the most gawd-awful commotion I've ever heard."

"Are you thirsty or hungry?" Cam asked.

"I drank the last of my water last night. The dog and I ate the last can of Vienna sausage yesterday."

"We've got cold water or Mountain Dew and some egg salad for sandwiches if you're hungry."

"I would be grateful for a soda and sandwich," Reba said.

Cam nodded to Sandy. "Will you tear up some jerky for the pup? Have you given him a name yet?" Cam rummaged through the cooler for a cold soda and handed it to Reba. "Here you go. I'll have a sandwich up in a bit. Sandy, do you want one?"

"No, I'm good." She was tearing the jerky into strips for the hungry pup.

"I haven't settled on a name yet. I've no place to go, so I don't know if I'd be able to keep him in a shelter. He's a little whippersnapper, though."

"Hey, there's your name. How do you do, Mr. Whip?" Sandy asked the pup, who was steadily chewing on the jerky in her hand.

"Yeah, Whip, I can remember that. He was a godsend and has kept me from going nuts waiting for help."

Cam handed her a sandwich filled with Wanda's delicious egg salad. "We have two options. We can take you into town if you need immediate attention, or you can ride with us for a bit. To be honest, we'd be grateful if you rode with us since you know the area and we don't."

Reba smiled up at Cam. "That's the least I can do for you gals. Where are you from?"

"Morganza," Cam answered.

"God bless you for coming to help strangers out," Reba said.

"Do you know many of the people in this area, Ms. Reba?" Cam asked.

"I've been here all of my sixty-five years, and I know most of the folks within miles of here. Mostly older people like me."

"Do you know who lived in the first home, a cinder block home we passed just a way back?" Sandy asked.

"Jack Johnson, but he's been in the hospital in Baton Rouge for a couple of weeks. He took a nasty spill and broke his hip."

"Who lives next down this way?" Cam asked, pointing farther down the river.

"Sally and Joe Morrison. They have lived there as long as I can remember."

"Do you know if they were home when the flood came?" Cam asked.

"I haven't seen anyone pass this way in days. Joe had an old aluminum boat, but I don't think he had a motor for it. Sally was teasing him about turning it into a flower garden the last I knew."

Cam looked up at Sandy. "Let's go see if we can find them. Hold on tight."

Sandy handed the pup to Cam, who sat beside Reba.

"You're a cute boy," Cam said as she scratched behind his ears. "It's going to be loud for a little bit."

When a small brick house came into view, Cam was relieved to see the older couple sitting on top of their home. Cam noticed a hole cut into the roof and assumed they had fled into the attic and then cut their way out when the water started rising.

"Well, I'll be damned. You two made it," Reba said when she spotted her friends. She waved and hollered to them. "You two all right?"

"We are now," Joe answered. "I seen 'em helicopters going over earlier, but I couldn't wave 'em down."

"You're in luck. These two angels have come to save us." Reba smiled at Cam.

Cam was scratching her head. "How we gonna get you two down from there?"

"I have a ladder on the back porch if it didn't get sucked away. We can climb down that if y'all can get it." Joe tried to stand and nearly toppled off the roof.

"You two sit tight, and we'll drive around back and see if we can get the ladder."

Sandy drove the boat into the backyard. When she suddenly let off the gas, Cam looked up to see what had stopped Sandy. A ten-foot gator was dozing in the sun blocking the back door. "Rev your engine, and let's see if we can scare him off."

Sandy held tight to the controls as she raced the engine. The loud rumble of the engine vibrating in the water startled the gator, and it made a prompt exit toward the river. Cam spotted the ladder just inside the door. She handed Whip to Reba.

"Keep an eye on him in case he decides to come back."

Sandy pulled out her pistol and checked the load. "All good, but watch out for snakes."

Cam stepped cautiously into the two feet of water in the yard, and it took several attempts to jerk the back door open.

When she was able, she reached inside and grabbed the ladder before racing back to the boat. "Got it."

Sandy drove the boat back to the front of the house and moved as close as possible. Cam set the ladder against the roofline and made sure it was secure.

"Let's get you two in the boat."

"Sally, you go first," Joe said. "Just scoot down on your butt. Don't try to stand up."

Sally inched her way to the edge of the roof with Joe right beside her. Cam guided her feet onto the ladder and held her arms as she climbed down.

"There you go." Cam recommended Sally sit beside Reba. "Ready, Mr. Joe?"

"On my way," he answered. Joe scrambled down the ladder like a much younger man. He took a seat across from the ladies.

"We have drinks and some egg salad if you'd like a sandwich," Sandy offered. She smiled at Cam when both requested a sandwich. Wanda would be proud of the compliments she received on the egg salad, even if Cam and Sandy's lunch was dwindling. Feeding the survivors who hadn't had a decent meal for days was much more critical. Cam pulled out two bottles of water for the couple and some caffeine for her and Sandy.

While Sandy made them sandwiches, Cam looked at Reba. "Who is next in the area?"

"Jimmy Freeman, about a half-mile farther down," Reba answered.

"Are you two willing for us going to check on him before we take you into town?" Cam asked.

"Oh yes, Jimmy is my fishing buddy," Joe said. "Lordy, I hope he's okay. He's had heart problems for years."

"Let's go," Cam said to Sandy with some urgency. She knew the flood trauma wasn't safe for anyone, much less someone with cardiac issues. "Wait, I've got to mark the door." Cam stepped out with the can of yellow paint and painted a checkmark, plus sign, and the number two on the door. When she stepped back into the boat, Cam grinned at Reba. "We were so excited to find you that we forgot to mark the door."

"We can do it on the way back," Sandy replied.

"What's the paint for?" Ms. Reba asked.

"It tells other search teams the house is clear," Cam said.

"That's a smart move," Joe replied.

Sandy picked up speed once she returned to the road where the water was still deep. When they approached the house, Sandy looked at Cam. "You want me to take this one?"

"No, I'm good." Cam stepped onto the front porch and pushed in the front door. The odor in the house told her what she had already feared. She waded through a foot of muddy water into a bedroom, just off the living area. Jimmy Freeman was stretched out on the bed, a peaceful smile covering his pale face. Cam checked, but his body was cold, and there was no sign of a pulse. She located a bedspread and covered the man's body.

She pulled the front door closed as tightly as possible and turned toward the boat.

Sandy knew by Cam's expression that Jimmy had not survived.

Cam looked at the three eager faces in the boat and shook her head. "I'm sorry, but Jimmy looks like he had a heart attack. He's stretched out on his bed, clutching a picture to his chest."

"That would be his wife, Molly, who died several years ago. He was probably smiling because she came to greet him."

Sandy handed Cam the can of red paint. She walked back to the door and drew a large red X and the number one. When she stepped back into the boat, she placed the paint back in the box. "Let's get these folks to town."

Sandy saw Cam wipe her eyes as they drove as fast as they could back into town. She was sure Cam would blame the wind rushing into her face for the tears, but Sandy knew better. Once they reached the command center, they got Joe and Sally situated with a volunteer. Cam reported Mr. Freeman's death as Sandy topped off the fuel in the boat. Reba was talking with Sally when Cam came to say goodbye.

"May I ask a favor?" Reba asked.

"Sure, anything?" Cam replied.

"Let me go with you to help. These are my people."

Cam could see the tears in her eyes. "What about Whip?"

"Sally and Joe will make sure he is cared for once they reach the shelter, and I'll join them later."

"Let's go then," Cam said.

They stopped off at the command center to get a pair of boots for Reba and then walked back to the airboat. Sandy smiled when she looked up to see Reba with Cam.

"We have a personal tour guide?"

"Something like that," Cam answered with a smile as Reba climbed into the boat.

Sandy patted Cam's shoulder. "Well, it does give us the advantage of her knowing where people live."

"That it does. Let's roll." Cam took a seat beside Sandy. "Sorry, we don't have another pair of ear protection."

"That's okay. I'm hard of hearing anyhow." Reba smiled.

Now that Sandy knew at least part of the route, the trip back was quicker. They stopped at Reba's to mark her door, and Cam offered her the can of paint. She watched Reba step onto her porch and said, "A check mark, plus one."

Reba painted the door and scrambled back to the boat. "The Morgan's are next. They are a young couple with a little girl, about a mile past Mr. Freeman."

Not long after they passed Mr. Freeman's house, they saw a small canoe moving toward them.

"There they are," Reba cried out when she saw them.

Sandy killed the motor, and they glided toward the canoe. Cam grabbed onto the edge of the canoe to steady them. "Is everyone okay?" she asked.

"We're alive, and right now, that's all that matters," Mr. Morgan said.

"Hungry and thirsty?" Cam asked.

"We could eat. I'd kill for a hot coffee about now," Mrs. Morgan said.

"Reba, will you make these folks a sandwich? I hope you like egg salad," Cam said. "I can't offer you coffee, but this may give you a caffeine kick." Cam gave her a Mountain Dew. We also have water if you'd prefer."

"A water for Maggie and me will be fine. Thank you so much," Mr. Morgan said. "I'm glad to see you, Ms. Reba."

"These two angels, Cam and Sandy, rescued me, Joe, and Sally this afternoon. Jimmy Freeman didn't make it."

"I'm sorry to hear that. Jimmy was a good man."

"He always gave me a chocolate bar," Maggie said.

"Are you strong enough to paddle for a while? We want to check at least a few more homes before the sun starts to fade," Cam said. "If you haven't made it into town, we can tow you the rest of the way."

"I can handle that now that I've got some calories to burn."

Sandy reached into the bag and pulled out some jerky sticks. "These should help and take a few water bottles. This humidity will suck you dry, and you'll be paddling against the current as the water is trying to make it back to the river."

"Tell me about it. It's taken me over an hour to make it this far."

Reba smiled at the young man. "You can stop off at my place and wait on my porch if you get tired. The trailer's pretty much gone, but the porch is solid."

"That sounds like a good plan. I think I can make it there. If not, I'll tie up to a tree and wait for you to come back through. I hope you find others."

"We hope so, too." Sandy smiled at Maggie. "I bet I've got something that will tickle your tummy." She pulled out the bag of brownies Wanda had made. "I left the cookies in the truck but was afraid these would melt." She handed them over a bag of brownies and handed one to Cam and Reba. "Ready?"

"Daylight's a wasting," Cam said. "We'll be back for you soon."

Sandy showed Maggie how to cover her ears with her hands. Then the engine roared to life, and the airboat sped away. Sandy looked at the map and saw how many dots were on the map. There was no way they would reach them all today. She slowed as they passed the Morgan home.

"There are so many homes left to check. There is no way we will reach them all today. Is there anyone particularly vulnerable close by we can reach within the next hour?"

Reba pointed to a house two spots down. "Myrtis Blackfoot is a brittle diabetic. We could check Myrtis and swing back by John and Beth Sewell's place."

Sandy nodded. "We can stop by briefly to see if the Sewell's are home and safe, then tell them we would return."

"On second thought, if she's home, let's pick them up. Beth is a trauma nurse and may be of help if Myrtis is in crisis."

"Good thinking. How far to the Sewell home?" Cam asked.

"Two miles or so," Reba answered.

"On it," Sandy said. "Hang on tight."

Several minutes later, Reba pointed out a log cabin tucked back in the woods. As they approached, they saw a man and woman sitting on the top deck around a grill.

"You folks look comfortable," Reba said.

"He's cooking the last of the hamburgers. Can y'all stop in for a bite?" Beth asked.

"We'd love nothing more, but I want to check on Myrtis and her sugar. You know she's a brittle diabetic," Reba said.

"Damn, I forgot about that. I'll be right down," Beth said.

"A burger to go, ladies?" John asked.

"They sure smell good, and I think these ladies have given away all their food to the folks they've rescued."

"Give me two minutes, and I'll have them ready. I just have ketchup."

"That's perfect," Cam said.

"On my way then," John said, and grabbed a plate of burgers before heading inside.

Beth stepped out of the front door in boots and carrying a small bag. "I found some of those powders we add to water for energy, but I don't have water."

"We've got that covered," Cam said and opened the cooler.

"I'd kill for one of those Dews," John said as he handed Sandy a plate of burgers.

Cam pulled out two and handed them to him. "We'll be back for you once we collect Myrtis."

"I'll toss some clean clothes in a bag and be ready," he told Beth and kissed her. "Good luck. I hope Myrtis is fine."

Sandy swallowed. "We'll be back soon. Thanks for the burgers."

"My pleasure. Thanks for the caffeine." John grinned back at her.

†

The deeper they drove away from town, the denser the trees grew. The environment reminded Sandy of the rear of the island back home. They often frequented the area to cull the wild hog population, but it could be a spooky place with all the hanging vines and thick bogs. It was difficult to tell where the riverbank usually was due to the immense flood water, but Sandy knew that when dry, the place would be beautiful. As she swallowed the last bite of a double hamburger, Sandy felt refreshed and energized. It had been a long and emotionally draining day, but successful none the least. They saved as many as they could, and she hoped their last stop would also be positive. When Reba signaled her,

Sandy eased off the accelerator to slow the boat. She saw the small home Reba pointed to and winced at several feet lapping the walls just below a first-floor window. The water was aggressively draining back toward the river and punishing anything in its path. Sandy wasn't sure how the tiny house had survived without being ripped from the foundation and sensed an even greater urgency than the medical concern.

When she pulled in front of the home, she turned to Cam. "We need to get her out as quickly as possible. I don't think the house can stand the force of the water much longer. It's at an odd angle like it's already begun to slide off the foundation."

"I see that now," Cam said. "Sharp eye, Sandy. Okay, ladies, we need to move quickly to get her out." Cam turned back to Sandy. "I won't tie off here in case we need to make a quick exit."

"I can hold the boat in place for a while," Sandy replied.

Cam nodded and stood from her seat. "We need to move quickly. This home isn't stable and easily could be washed off the foundation into the river."

Beth had already put a powder mixture in a bottle of water. She looked at Reba. "Let's go get Myrtis."

Cam stepped off the boat onto the small porch. She could feel the wood shifting under her feet. "Hurry now, but step safely," Cam said as she extended her hand to Beth, then Reba. "The first order of business is to get her into the boat. You can triage once she's safely out of that home. Grab what she needs, and let's all make it safely out."

Reba pushed through the door and waded through the water to reach Myrtis who was stretched out on a sofa, the water mere inches from where she rested. At first, Cam worried they had arrived too late. The frail woman was pale and not moving, but when Reba called out to her, the woman's eyes shot open.

"Reba," she said. "What are you doing here?"

"We've come to take you out of here. The flood has damaged the house, and you need to move now." Reba looked at Myrtis, who struggled to sit up. "Can you stand?"

"No, I fell twice getting here. My legs keep giving out on me." Myrtis began shedding tears.

"It's going to be okay," Cam said. "I'll get her to the boat if you get her medical supplies and whatever you can."

"Myrtis, where's your test kit? Do you have any insulin left?" Beth asked.

"I used my last dose yesterday, but I'm not sure if it was effective. The power has been out for two days, and I wasn't able to keep it refrigerated."

"That's okay," Beth patted her arm, "We'll take good care of you."

Cam looked at Reba. "Y'all get her medicines and medical supplies and anything else she might need, and I'll get her to the boat."

"Get her started sipping the water I made, and we'll be right behind you," Beth answered.

Cam could feel the floor swaying beneath their feet. "Please hurry. We need to get out of here soon." Cam bent down and scooped the frail woman in her arms. "Hang on. We'll be out in a second."

"Reba, please grab my dentures and glasses off the bedside table," Myrtis weakly called out.

"Yes, ma'am," Reba answered.

Cam waded back to the door and carefully stepped onto the porch. Sandy smiled when she saw Cam. "Is she okay?"

"She will be soon." Cam walked toward the boat. "I don't think I can safely step into the boat with her. Can you hold her in your arms, Squirt?"

"She can't be worse than wrestling an alligator," Sandy teased.

"You wrestle alligators?" Myrtis asked.

Sandy beamed with pride. "Yes, ma'am. My sisters and I harvest them every gator season. It's our family business."

Myrtis smiled. "Why, you're no bigger than a minute. How can you do that?"

Cam chuckled. "She may be the runt of the litter, but she's strong as an ox and bull-headed to boot." Cam eased Myrtis into Sandy's arms.

"I've got her," Sandy said and eased her into a seat.

Cam held the boat in place. "See if you can get some small sips of water into her. I've got the boat steadied." Cam could feel the water pressure on the boat and knew that Sandy's arms must have been screaming from the exertion of holding the vessel in place. She was smaller than the rest of her sisters, but Sandy was tough as nails. "I hope they hurry."

Sandy knelt next to Myrtis. "You heard the lady, small sips." Sandy heard a loud creak and knew the house could go at any minute. She could already see daylight through some of the loose boards.

Cam saw the house begin to sway. "Beth, we need to go now," Cam hollered.

"On our way," Beth called back, and Cam was relieved to see them exit the front door.

She helped them back into the boat and looked at Sandy. "Get us out of here." Cam released the railing she was holding to steady the craft and took a seat beside Sandy as she eased the boat away from the porch.

"I radioed ahead for medical attention. I'll come back for John," Sandy said to Beth.

"He'll be fine." Beth smiled.

They had barely made it fifty yards when they saw the wood-frame home collapse on itself, and the water dragged it toward the river. The airboat's engine muffled the sound, and Myrtis was looking away as her home disappeared from view, taking her belongings into the angry, muddy water. She had escaped with her life and could replace material objects, but Sandy worried about the pain that losing so many sentimental items would have on Myrtis.

Myrtis looked weak as Beth continued to offer small sips of the sugary liquid. Sandy could see the worry in Beth's eyes and accelerated as fast as she felt safe. She slowed momentarily to shout to John that she would be back for him, and he nodded in confirmation.

Sandy was relieved when she made the final turn toward the command center to see an ambulance waiting for their arrival. She didn't think Myrtis could have grown paler, but she had during the short ride. The boat floated to a stop, and Cam picked Myrtis up and handed her off to the paramedics.

Beth turned to Sandy. "Tell John I'm going to ride into my hospital with Myrtis and ask him to meet me there. I left my Jeep there, and if we're lucky, it didn't get flooded."

"We'll make sure he gets there," Sandy replied.

Reba stepped out of the boat with some assistance. Cam smiled at her. "These gentlemen will get you to the command center and get you to temporary housing. Thank you for all your help today."

"God bless the two of y'all for coming to save us," Reba said. "Will I see you before you go?"

"That's always a possibility." Sandy smiled. "If not, here is one of our cards, so you can keep in touch."

Reba took the card. "Stay safe."

Cam nodded and turned to Sandy. "Let's go get John."

Sandy nodded and waited for Reba to step away, then for Myrtis and Beth to disappear into the ambulance, then she slowly turned the boat around.

As they were heading back, Sandy slowed the boat and then killed the engine. "What's up?" Cam asked.

"We have another survivor," Sandy answered and pointed to a tiny black kitten clinging to the branch of a tree ten feet above the water. "Looks like I'm going for a climb."

Cam smiled and grabbed a branch to steady the boat. "I'll try to hold it as best I can."

Sandy nodded. "If you need to, crank it up and circle until I come back down."

"Just be careful. I don't need to fish you both out of this mess," Cam warned with a smirk.

Sandy climbed into the tree and crept out onto the smaller limb where the terrified kitten was clinging to the branch. "Come here, little one," Sandy gently coaxed the kitten. Bright green eyes stared back at her, and a weak mewl greeted her as she drew close. "Come here," she repeated and held her hand out to the animal.

The kitten took a tentative step toward Sandy then froze when the sound of a tree limb cracking filled the air. Sandy called down to Cam. "Please tell me that didn't come from this tree?"

"No, it didn't, but y'all need to make it quick. We have unwelcome company coming our way," Cam replied.

Sandy looked up to see past the end of the boat. A large gator was swimming toward them. Sandy knew she needed to grab the kitten and get down out of the tree before one or both of them became his dinner. "You're going to have to trust me," Sandy said and reached out with quick reflexes to snag the kitten from the limb.

"Gotcha," she said and stroked the kitten's head.

"Y'all can get acquainted later after we get some distance between Bubba Gump's cousin and us," Cam said as she nodded toward the big gator.

"Damn, he is a big boy," Sandy cried out. "Too bad we're out of season." Sandy tucked the kitten inside her work shirt and scrambled back down the tree. Cam steadied the boat while she dropped in and took the driver's seat. The kitten poked his head through two buttons and snuggled next to Sandy.

"Let's go get John."

The boat engine roaring to life caused the gator to submerge, so Sandy carefully pulled away from the tree. A gator that size could quickly flip the light airboat if it hit the right spot. As soon as Sandy felt like she was beyond the gator, she sped up and away from the beast.

John was sitting in a rocker on his front porch when they returned. "How is Myrtis?"

"She'll be fine. There was an ambulance waiting for us when we got to town. Beth rode with her to the hospital and asked that you meet her there."

John smiled. "Yeah, she was smart enough to leave her Jeep. I just hope it didn't get flooded."

"We can give you a ride over if you need," Cam offered.

"I'll make it over there. It's not far from where you described the command center, so I can walk it if necessary."

Cam shook her head. "That's not necessary. We can load up and drive you over."

"I see you found another survivor," John said, pointing at the kitten.

"A big ole gator will have to find a different snack today," Sandy said and scratched the kitten's head.

"What you gonna name him? Or her?" John asked.

"We were in such a rush we didn't check. I'm not sure it's even old enough to tell yet." Sandy pulled the kitten from her shirt. "I do believe we have a little tomcat," she grinned. "River cat."

John chuckled. "Why not Amite? That's the name of the river trying to swallow him up?"

"I like that. Are you ready to become a bayou kitty, Amite?" Sandy started laughing when the kitten meowed in response. "I'll take that as a yes."

When Sandy paused leaving John and Beth's yard, Cam looked at her. Sandy's eyes were searching farther down their path, looking to see if they saw anything else moving. She looked back at Cam.

"I know what you're thinking, but it's already gonna be full dark when we make it in. We'll be ready to head out first light in the morning. Don't forget we still have to tow the Morgans the rest of the way also."

"Damn, I had forgotten they were waiting at Reba's," Sandy said. "Let's go before these mosquito's threaten to carry us off."

Sandy wasted no time getting them to Ms. Reba's. The Morgans were lounging on her front porch. "Sorry, it took us so long," Cam said. "We had a medical issue to deal with."

"Ms. Myrtis?" the young man asked. "We saw you go flying by."

"Yes, but she's going to be okay," Cam assured them. "Let's get you, folks, back to dry land. You want to leave your canoe or have us tow you?"

"I reckon it will be safe here. Once we get to town, we won't have any place to store it."

"Does your house look pretty solid? We could tow it back out there tomorrow and store it for you," Sandy offered.

The young man's smile lit up his face. "That would be great. Towing it now would only slow us down. To be honest, I'm ready for something hot to eat and a cot to lay down on."

"I can understand that," Sandy said. "Grab your bags, and let's go."

When they arrived at the command center, they were surprised to find Beth waiting for them. "The Jeep was in good shape, and Myrtis is under observation overnight, so I thought I'd come to pick you up. Your brother called the hospital and left word for us to crash with them. They were spared from the flooding and are waiting for us." She looked at Cam and Sandy. "They have room for two more if you'd care to join us."

"It's a bit of a drive, but you could have a hot shower and warm bed," John tossed in.

"Thanks, but we're going to hang out here and get an early jump in the morning," Cam said.

Beth nodded. "Thank you both for all that you have done for all of us. I'm not sure how much longer Myrtis would have made it if you hadn't arrived. I hope if you make it back under different circumstances, you will drop in and see us."

Sandy smiled. "She would have had one wild ride to Nawlins for sure. I'm glad we got her out before the house collapsed."

"It what?" John said.

"Collapsed and was pulled into the river minutes after we got her out," Beth explained.

"Oh, my goodness. That's too close for comfort." John hugged his wife. "Thank you for bringing her back safe to me."

"Stay safe, and I hope you can start cleaning up soon. There are a lot of people that will need help," Sandy said as she shook his hand.

"Take care of Amite," he chuckled.

"Who?" Beth asked, confused.

Sandy opened her shirt for Beth to see the kitten. "Our first four-legged rescue."

"Aww. How adorable."

"He was clinging to a tree limb for dear life, trying his best not to become gator bait." Sandy scratched under his neck, and he immediately began purring loudly.

"Stay safe, and thanks again for all your help." Beth took John by the hand, and they walked over to her Jeep.

"You want to fuel up or load the boat first?" Cam asked.

"I'll refuel it and load it onto the trailer. Then we've got to find out what that delicious smell is filling the air."

"My mouth has been watering since we arrived. I am so ready for some hot food," Cam replied. "It looks like it's going to be a clear night. There's a large empty parking lot over by the theater. Do you want to blow up a mattress and toss our sleeping bags in the bed of the truck?"

"I think that's why they call it a bed. It's been a long time since we've slept out under the stars together," Sandy replied.

"We were both much smaller and younger, then," Cam said. "Let's do it."

After loading the airboat, Cam and Sandy followed their noses to the food tent. There they were loaded up with boxes of fried chicken wings, macaroni and cheese, garlic toast, and about a half of a caramel cake.

"Any more, and we'll need a wagon to haul all of this food," Cam replied when a woman tried to hand her more food. She took several packets of plastic dinnerware and a roll of paper towels.

"You two worked hard today, and from what we've heard, you gave away the lunch you packed and your snacks to the folks you rescued. It's our only way of saying thanks."

"Would you have any milk or anything soft for our newest team member?" Sandy asked, pointing to Amite poking his head out of her shirt.

"How adorable. I've got some powdered milk and a can of deviled ham. If you come in for breakfast, I'll bring him some kitten food."

"That would be awesome," Sandy replied. She took the bowl and food items offered.

"Do you ladies have drinks?"

"Yes, ma'am, I believe we are all set. Thank you," Cam replied.

"I'm Charlotte. I'll see you ladies in the morning. I'm making pancakes at five." she smiled.

"We're Cam and Sandy," Cam replied. "We will see you in the morning."

They loaded the food into the truck and drove over to the empty parking lot. "This should do well," Cam said. An RV parked a hundred yards away. "Looks like we weren't the only ones with this idea."

"Let's grub, and then we can set up our bed." Sandy took Amite's bowl and made up some milk. Then she spread some of the ground meat into the bowl and sat it in front of him while Cam set up their meal on the tailgate.

They both laughed at the sound Amite made as he dug into the food. A cross between a purr and a growl could be heard as he buried his face in the mixture.

"No telling how long it's been since he ate," Sandy said as she watched him.

"I know how long it's been since we ate," Cam teased and handed Sandy a fork.

Sandy and Cam devoured the mound of chicken wings along with most of the mac and cheese. Amite got in on the action, chewing on some chicken bones with bits of meat left for him to eat.

"As good as that cake looks, I can't eat another bite," Cam said.

"Right now, but two hours from now may be a different story." Sandy tossed Cam a fresh soda.

"That's true. Let's pick up our trash and get our bed set up," Cam suggested.

Cam sat on the cooler and watched Sandy and Amite play after they had the food stored and bed set up. The moon had risen, and with little traffic, the night filled with the sounds of the bayou.

"Seems odd to hear these sounds in the city," Sandy said as she sat beside Cam.

"Mother Nature's reminder that she's still the most powerful creation, and with other events like this one, she could reclaim much of what she's lost to humans."

Sandy nodded. "That's a scary thought. But you're right, first Hurricane Katrina, now these floods. It reminds us how fragile we are."

"Hey, look. I think Amite's about ready to call it a night." The kitten had found a patch of sand and was burying his deposit. "I think I'll take a walk to the porta-potty and hit the mattress," Cam said.

"I'll go once you return. You and Amite can't hog the whole bed, though," Sandy teased.

"We'll try not to. Be back in a few."

CHAPTER FIVE

The sound of helicopter rotors woke Cam the next morning, and she looked over to find Amite snuggled against Sandy's neck. She grabbed her camera and snapped a quick picture. The sound of the camera shutter caught Amite's attention, and the sparkling green eyes popped open. The kitten stretched his front paws and nuzzled into Sandy's neck.

Sandy reached over to pick up the kitten. "Good morning to you too," she whispered to him and looked over to see Cam watching them. "Good morning, Cam."

"Morning. Are you ready to rock and roll today?"

"After some pancakes and a potty break, heck yeah," Sandy answered.

"You can use the facilities first, and I'll get the little man here started on some breakfast," Cam said as she slid down to the tailgate and slipped her boots on.

"Thanks, Cam." Sandy settled Amite on the tailgate, put her boots on, and started toward the porta-potty.

Amite watched her go and started meowing. "It's okay. She'll be right back. Let's get you some breakfast." Cam sat the kitten on her shoulder as she made some powdered milk and canned meat mix for him. "Here you go, big boy," Cam said as she laid the bowl on the tailgate. Amite began eating while Cam brushed her teeth and ran a brush through her hair. She dressed in a clean work shirt and T-shirt. Cam was pulling on her hat when Sandy returned.

"That was quick."

"I thought I'd never make it in time," Sandy grinned. "My bladder was screaming halfway there."

"I know that feeling. Do you want to meet me at the food tent?"

"Sounds like a deal. I'll pull the bed cover up and secure it if it rains, and drive the truck around by the tent."

"I'll see you in a few then," Cam said.

Sandy brushed her hair and teeth, then rinsed out Amite's bowl. "Do you need to potty?" Sandy picked him up and carried him to a grassy area.

"You are such a good boy," she praised when he covered up his business and came bouncing back to her.

Sandy secured the bed cover and tucked Amite into her shirt. "Let's roll."

As promised, Charlotte and several other ladies were cooking pancakes, bacon, and scrambled eggs when Cam and Sandy arrived at the food tent.

"It smells heavenly in here," Sandy said as she entered.

"You two are the first up and about, but we have food ready if you are," Charlotte answered.

"I can't believe we were hungry after that feast last night, but the smell has my mouth watering," Cam returned with a smile.

"I also brought a few things for Amite," Charlotte said. "I had some extras around the house." She handed a bag of goodies to Sandy.

Sandy opened the bag to find food and water bowls, a small bag of dry food, and a few cans of wet kitten food. She laughed when she spotted a collar and two balls with bells inside them. She looked up at Charlotte with tears in her eyes.

"Thank you so much." Sandy pulled out the tiny red collar and placed it around his neck. "Don't you look handsome?"

"He certainly does. You are more than welcome. Both of you," Charlotte said and reached over to pet Amite's head. "Let me change gloves, and I'll get you plates started."

"Already on it," a voice called out, and Sandy looked up to see Ms. Reba.

"Hey, stranger. How are you?" Sandy asked.

"I'm happy to be alive. I volunteered to help out, and Charlotte picked me up this morning. Turns out she's got an extra room in her home that she's going to let me use for a bit."

"That's fantastic news," Cam replied.

"It'll be nice to have her company and great to help out a neighbor in need," Charlotte added.

"Here you go, ladies. One of the men set up a small table to use to eat on. What can I get you to drink?"

"I'd love some juice and coffee if you have it, Ms. Reba," Cam answered.

"Apple or orange?"

"Apple, please."

"You too, Sandy?" Reba asked.

"Yes, please," Sandy answered and filled her mouth with a bite of eggs.

Reba delivered the drinks. "We have some lunch bags made up with sandwiches and chips if y'all want to take a few. There's something extraordinary planned for tonight."

"Do tell," Sandy said.

"Charlotte has arranged for Duke's to provide supper. They will grill some of their famous oysters, do a shrimp boil, and all the fixins to go with them."

"Aww, man, I love Duke's," Cam said. "Wait until you taste their oysters. Good job, Ms. Charlotte."

"Huh," Charlotte said from her spot at the grill.

"I was telling them about the dinner you have arranged for tonight," Reba said.

Charlotte smiled at them. "Oh, it wasn't hard to convince them to do it. Dukes were glad to help all you folks coming to help out. The owner used to be part of the Cajun Navy in his younger days, so he knows what you're doing firsthand."

"We're glad to do whatever we can," Cam replied.

"Reba tells me you gals hunt alligators. Is that right?" Charlotte asked.

Sandy piped up with a smile. "Yes, ma'am, since we were knee-high to a grasshopper. Dad taught all five of us girls to hunt and fish, and that's one of our main sources of income."

"That's amazing. You don't hear of too many women in that line of work," Charlotte said.

"You will as the industry keeps growing. The gators multiply faster than we can catch them," Cam said with a chuckle. "We own a small part of an island, too, and are infested with wild hogs. Every year during the holidays, we hunt to cull the growing population and roast them for families in our community."

"You are truly angels," Ms. Reba said.

"No, ma'am, we were taught to help out others when we can. Removing some wild hogs helps us maintain our property and feeds some families in need," Cam explained. "Many of them repay us in kindness by sharing crops they grow in their gardens."

"God bless ya'll. I'd better get back to work. I see some hungry men on the way. Stay safe today." Ms. Reba brought them four bags of lunch and sat them on the table.

"Thanks. Will we see you tonight?" Sandy asked.

"I'll be right here," Reba answered.

Cam and Sandy finished eating. "Thanks for a great breakfast and lunch," Sandy said as they made their way to the truck.

They sat in the cab for a few minutes studying the map. "I reckon we have a dozen more families to check today," Sandy said. She marked the Morgan family safe on her chart.

"Let's go see who we can find," Cam said.

†

They were amazed by how quickly the water was draining back toward the river. Sandy guessed the water level to be down six to eight inches from the previous day. "If the water keeps draining like this, we probably won't be needed after today," she said to Cam.

"I agree. It's been a good experience for us, though."

"Yes, it has. It's hard to imagine the difficult time it will be for some of these folks to move on with all the damages to their homes and lives. It's heartwarming to see the community supporting one another so well, so that may be the saving grace." Sandy smiled at Cam. "Thanks for letting us become a part of this."

Cam grinned. "No problem. Now that we have our feet wet, maybe we can help out in future disasters. If there is one thing for certain, this won't be the last big event."

"Hey, have you called home or that sexy deputy yet?" Sandy teased.

"Nope, I haven't. Why don't you call Wanda, and I'll try Luce?" Cam suggested. "Then we can hit the trail."

"Sounds good." Sandy pulled out her phone and walked a short distance.

Cam dialed Luce's cell phone and was happy she answered quickly. "Hey, did I catch you at a bad time?"

"No, I'm just heading out on patrol," Luce answered. "How are you two holding up?"

"We had a long day yesterday and will have another today, but the water is receding quickly, so we should be home soon."

"Has it been a good experience for y'all?" Luce asked.

"It has, and we've helped some great people to safety. I always wish we could do more, but they've been exceptionally appreciative of our assistance. Oh, we have a new family member, too."

"How did that happen?" Luce asked with a chuckle.

"Eagle-eye Sandy spotted a kitten clinging for his life on a branch last night, so she climbed up to get him to prevent him from being a gator snack."

"Have you seen many gators? I imagine the wildlife is all riled up right now."

"A few good-sized gators, some water moccasins, possums, and a raccoon. There's definitely at least one skunk in the area."

Luce broke out laughing. "They are hard to miss, aren't they?"

"Yes, they are." Cam loved the sound of Luce's laughter. "Do you have your weekend schedule yet?"

"Yes, I'm going to be off all of Sunday if you'd like some company," Luce offered.

"That sounds great. I'll give you a call when we get home, if not sooner, and we can plan the grand tour."

"Sounds good. I've missed not seeing you around town," Luce replied.

"I've missed you, too, but I will see you soon."

"Goodbye, Cam."

"See ya, Deputy," Cam answered, bringing another chuckle from Luce.

Cam hung up to find Sandy watching her. "All is well on the home front, I presume?"

"Yes, she'll be coming out Sunday when she's off duty."

"That sounds promising. Everything is good at home. Wanda was excited that we may be home soon."

"I bet she's been busy since we've been gone."

Sandy laughed. "The phone's been ringing off the hook for shine orders. She's got the mash started, but it looks like we'll need to cook a few nights."

"That's always a good problem to have." Cam stowed her phone. "Ready?"

"Waiting on you." Sandy grinned at Cam.

Their progress into the community was a much slower ride as the receding waters had filled the road with debris that Sandy had to maneuver around carefully. When they reached the first destination, Cam stepped onto the front stoop and found the home empty. There was no sign of the inhabitants. She checked the back of the house and called out several times but received no answer. She marked the front door and climbed back onto the boat. "Nobody home, and no sign they had been there recently."

"I didn't see any vehicle, so maybe they made it out safely," Sandy replied.

"Let's hope." Cam returned to her seat. "On to the next."

It was several miles before they would reach the next home site. The animals were returning to the area, and they saw evidence of the water's power everywhere. Buildings were crushed and pushed off foundations, and when Sandy pointed out a vehicle, Cam nodded. It was crushed like an empty soda can and wrapped around a tree, but they would need to check the car for occupants. The smell of death greeted them ten feet from the vehicle.

Cam covered her face with a bandana and motioned for Sandy to follow suit as the boat hovered near the car. Cam stood on the edge of the boat and glimpsed into the car, turned on its side. Inside, she could see two older men sprawled across the seats. There was no sign of life inside, and Cam turned quickly away. She stepped down onto the floor of the airboat.

Sandy watched her closely.

"Two older men are inside. They probably drowned while trying to escape. Radio it into command central. There's nothing we can do here."

Cam listened as Sandy radioed in their findings and current location. Woody replied that a National Guard Humvee dispatch would recover the victims.

"Let's get out of here," Cam said. "I need some fresh air."

Sandy swung the airboat back onto the road and watched Cam. Sandy knew Cam was taking the lead on searching to protect her from seeing potential dead bodies, but the loss of life touched even Cam. Sandy picked up as much speed as she dared to help clear the smell and memory from Cam's face.

When they arrived at the next stop, Sandy was relieved to see two women sitting on their front porch. "Well, looky at that, Sister, the cavalry has arrived, and it's two women."

"Yep, I see that, Margo. Young'uns too."

"Good morning, dear ladies," Cam said. "My sister Sandy and I would like to offer you a ride into town." Cam smiled up at the two women.

"Teresa and Margo LeBeau," the first lady offered. "We've been sitting here watching everything go floating by and hoping someone would come our way."

"Is it just the two of you?" Cam asked.

"Yes, we old widows have lived here for ten years together," Margo answered.

"Is the house in good shape?" Sandy asked.

"Aside from having no electric and losing all our food, we're okay. It's too dang hot to stay inside, and my stomach's been growling for days," Teresa replied.

"That we can help with right away," Cam said. "If you'll just climb aboard, we'll get you something to eat and be on our way." Cam cocked her head. "Is there anything inside you need to bring?"

"Dammit to hell, we were about to forget our suitcases, Margo," Teresa said. They stood in unison and walked inside, returning moments later with small identical suitcases.

Cam loaded them in the boat and assisted each of the women into a seat. "I'm not exactly sure what kind of sandwiches we have, but maybe they will hit the spot."

"I'm so hungry right now I could eat the backside of a mule," Margo commented.

"Well, we certainly don't have that." Sandy grinned as she handed Cam two of the bagged lunches. "Water or sodas?"

"A cold bit of water would be fine," Teresa said.

Sandy pulled two bottles from the cooler and handed them to the women.

"What's that poking outta your shirt, girl?" Margo asked.

"Amite. He's a lost soul we rescued from the jaws of a big alligator last night," Sandy said, elaborating on the rescue adventure.

"Really? How exciting," Teresa said. "Oh, ham and cheese, my favorite, potato chips, and a cookie too. Thank you, ladies."

"You're more than welcome," Cam said. "You are our first stop today. Would you mind riding along with us for a little bit to check on others before we head to town?"

"Not at all. The Wilson brothers came by three days ago and tried to get us to go, but the water was running way faster than our liking, so we decided to wait it out here." Teresa looked at Margo for confirmation.

Cam shot Sandy a knowing look. The Wilson brothers were probably the two men they had found in the car. The last thing these ladies needed to see was two dead friends being carried away in a body bag. Cam picked up a can of paint. "I hope you don't mind, but I have to paint a sign on your door, so other rescuers know you've already left. Is that okay?"

"Sure, we're gonna need a new paint job after this anyhow," Margo replied.

Cam spray painted the checkmark and happily added *plus two* on the door. A little positivity, but it did little to shred the memory of the dead men in the car. Cam seriously doubted they could have reached them in time to save them as fast as the water had been moving to crush the car that way.

"Who's the next neighbor down the line?" Sandy asked.

"That would have been the Wilsons, and the Martins are next about four miles on down the line." Teresa smiled. "The

Martins are a young couple. No kids yet, but I think he's a bootlegger. The word is he makes some fine shine."

Cam chuckled. "Word is, or have y'all sampled for yourselves?"

Teresa blushed. "Timothy may have dropped by a quart bottle of some watermelon shine."

"Nothing wrong with that. I hear it's good for your constitution," Cam teased.

"If that ain't for dang sure. Burned almost as much coming out as it did on the way down." Margo groaned and held her belly with a laugh.

"The proof was too high. Martin should a proofed it down some," Sandy blurted out without thinking.

"Now, how would a fine young lady like you know that?" Teresa asked with a wink.

"I musta seen it on the television or something," Sandy winked back.

"Right, well, it packed a mighty punch. We could sip on a shot glass of it all night long while playing cards," Teresa said. "Mighty fine tingling it gave you, too, once it hit your belly."

"It's going to be a bit loud," Sandy warned, then cranked the engine. She pulled away from the house slowly and went in search of the moonshiner. Sandy proceeded slowly while the women ate. She hoped the National Guard would have come and gone to collect the Wilson brothers before they started back to town.

Amite, tired from all the noise, decided to curl up inside Sandy's shirt for a nap. She could feel his warmth and the vibration of his purrs against her stomach. Once the women finished eating, Sandy picked up speed, craftily dodging debris in the roadway. "The water is going down fast now," she called out to Cam.

"I bet they opened some spillways farther south to draw down some of the water," Cam answered. They began seeing spots in the path where they could see the asphalt starting to shine up at them. "Our next stop may be our last," Cam said.

"That would be fine with me. Maybe we can load up and find a nice hot shower before dinner tonight." Sandy lifted her arm and made a face.

"I know. I could use one, too," Cam answered. "That way, we could be relatively fresh for the ride home tomorrow."

"Yeah, I don't think there's much left for us to do here," Sandy agreed. "We can go home and get ready for gator season."

Cam smiled. "Just a few more weeks, and you'll be ready for a week or two off."

"You got that right, but we'll have more money in the bank, and I can get back to fishing."

Cam nodded. Ever since Squirt was big enough to hold a cane pole, she would spend as much time fishing as she could. Sandy had made a lucrative side business of catching the giant catfish that were plentiful in the bayou. She would catch and drop them off for processing. She didn't have to spend countless hours skinning cats when there was the machinery and workforce to do it in minutes. The family was fortunate to make a good living doing the things in life they loved most.

A large coon hound waded across the front yard of the tiny home they approached. A man heard the approach of the engine and stepped out of the house carrying a shotgun. When he saw the sisters sitting in the boat, his tense body language relaxed.

"Hello," Cam called out to him, still a few yards from the house. "We are only here to help if needed."

"I'm sorry, but you never know when looters arrive these days. I remember what happened after Katrina, and we ain't got much, but I'd like to keep what we have." He lowered the gun. "I'm Timothy."

"Sandy and Cam," Cam pointed out. "I assume you know these two," she grinned, pointing at the sisters.

"Yes'm, I do believe so. You gotta watch these two if you play poker with the sisters, or they'll cheat you right out of your breeches."

"Sounds like a sore loser to me," Margo cackled. "How's the missus?"

"She's about to pop. She's due next month, but I swear she grows ornerier every day." The missus, Caroline Martin, shuffled out the front door, extremely pregnant.

"Oh, my goodness," Margo said. "Honey, you look downright miserable."

"That's cause I am, Ms. Margo. I'm glad to see you two are safe."

"Would you like a ride into town? The water is receding, but I'm not sure how safe it is to stay without power. Especially with a baby on the way," Cam said.

"Heck yes," Caroline said. "Grab our go bags, Tim, and let's get outta here."

"Can we take Roscoe?" Tim asked, pointing to the dog.

"Of course, we can," Cam said. "Let's get your lady settled, and you can grab bags and Roscoe. "Have you eaten lately?"

"The last of our food ran out last night. Tim hasn't eaten for days, saying me and the baby needed it more." Caroline eased down onto a seat.

"We've got some lunch bags with sandwiches, chips, and a cookie we can offer." Sandy handed Cam the last two bags. "We've got cold water and Mountain Dews, too."

"I'd love me a Dew," Tim said as he sat two bags in the boat then called to Roscoe. He gently lifted the dog onto the front of the craft. "Stay," he commanded. Roscoe sat immediately. Tim wiped his wet hands on his jeans and took a cold bottle from Cam. "Thanks."

"No problem. We'll ease on out while y'all begin eating," Sandy told them.

The young couple tore into the food with eagerness.

"Man, this tastes good," Tim said. "I have a brother in town, if we can just make it there, we can stay with him until the baby arrives, or it's safe to go home."

"We'll get you there. Have you talked to your brother, so he knows you're okay?" Margo asked.

"Not in a few days. Our battery went dead," Tim replied. "He told us someone would be coming soon."

Cam reached into her pocket and handed him her phone. "We will be at the command center on O'Neal Lane in thirty minutes or so."

"Thanks," Tim replied and made a quick call to his brother. "He'll meet us there," he told Caroline.

Cam looked up ahead and saw the damaged car coming up on the right. She knew Tim had seen it also, and Cam quickly shook her head in the hope he wouldn't point it out to the sisters. She had intentionally positioned the sisters on the side of the boat where they couldn't see the car. Tim frowned but nodded his understanding of her unspoken message. He spoke to Caroline to distract her as well.

Once Sandy passed the car, she began to speed up. "Hold on, Roscoe," she called out.

Twenty minutes later, they floated to a stop at the command center. Tim helped Caroline onto the solid ground while Cam and Sandy assisted the sisters.

After they had everyone unloaded, Woody came over to them. "How's it looking out there?"

"The Martin's place is the farthest we could make it. The water is receding quickly. Did the Wilson brothers get picked up?"

"Yes, they did. I'm sorry y'all had to witness that."

"I just hate we were too late to help, but it appears they had been there for a few days." Cam shrugged her shoulders. "A shame, though, to die like that."

"Yeah, it is. Oh, Beth said for you to give her a call. She's made arrangements for you two to have a nice hot shower tonight." Woody grinned. "She's over at the hospital until seven." He handed Cam the number.

"I reckon we'll get loaded up and go get a shower. I sure could use one." Cam replied.

"That makes two of us. I'm beginning to offend myself," Sandy chuckled.

"Ms. Reba has volunteered to babysit while you ladies get cleaned up," Woody said before turning away.

Sandy drove the boat onto the trailer, and they stored the cooler and supplies. Cam gave Beth a call, and she told them to come on over and enter through the Emergency Room entrance.

Sandy went in search of Ms. Reba. "I hear you volunteered to babysit," Sandy said when she found her.

Ms. Reba smiled as she reached for Amite. "Yes, I'd love to."

"Just don't spoil him too bad while I'm gone." Sandy winked at her.

"I'll try my best. Duke's will be here soon to start cooking, and I've got it on good intel that they are also bringing a cold keg of beer."

"That sounds great. Is there anything we can do to help out?" Sandy asked.

85

"Nope, they are bringing plenty of help with them. They have one of the world's fastest oyster shuckers working for them, ya know. I've lost count of how many contests he's won."

"I reckon I'd better sit and watch, then, and maybe learn a few tips." Sandy grinned at Ms. Reba. "We'll be back soon."

"Take your time. We'll be right here waiting."

Sandy scratched under Amite's chin. "You be a good boy. I'll be back in a bit."

Sandy returned to the truck where Cam was just finishing a call. "The sexy deputy?" she teased.

"No, I called her first. That was Wanda. I told her we would be home before lunch tomorrow."

Sandy buckled in. "Do you want to try to cook tomorrow night?"

"Might as well get a jump on it. Maybe we can take a run down to meet the Texas buyer and a few local runs." Cam started the truck. "It sounds like people are getting mighty thirsty."

"That's always a good thing to hear. Good money from thirsty customers."

"Whatcha say we go get cleaned up?" Cam said.

"I'm so ready for a nice, long, hot shower."

"Me too," Cam responded and put the truck in gear.

When they entered the emergency room, Cam and Sandy were surprised by a round of applause from the hospital staff. Beth had told her coworkers of the sister team that had come to their rescue and the good deeds they had done for the community. The hospital workers greeted Cam and Sandy with handshakes and appreciation for their hard work. Sandy was overwhelmed by the outpouring of thanks from strangers.

"You're welcome," she repeated. "We were glad to do what we could to help."

Cam stepped back and allowed Sandy to be in the forefront. "How's Myrtis?" she asked Beth.

"She's fine and went to a family member's home earlier this morning. She doesn't remember much of yesterday but said to thank you ladies for saving her."

"I'm glad to hear that. Myrtis had me worried," Cam admitted.

"We got there in the nick of time. If her sugar didn't do her in, the collapse of the house surely would have," Beth replied.

Cam looked worried. "Do you think she'll be able to rebuild?"

"With some federal assistance and good neighbors," Beth smiled. "John is already working with FEMA to get her set up for aid."

Cam nodded. "You got a good man there."

"I think I'll keep him around for a bit." Beth chuckled. "He wants to go home tomorrow and survey damages."

Cam ran a hand through her hair. "That shouldn't be a problem as fast as the water is receding. We couldn't make it any farther than the Martins today."

"We heard about the Wilson brothers. Did you find them?"

Cam felt the tears well up in her eyes. "Yes, but we were days too late in reaching them."

"You two did everything you could for this community. Be proud of your accomplishments and the families you helped." Beth laid a comforting hand on Cam's shoulder. "The doctors' lounge only has one shower, but it's private. Should we go rescue Sandy so y'all can get cleaned up?"

Cam chuckled. "She looks a bit nervous, so now would be a good time."

"Let's go, then." Beth motioned to Sandy and took them to the lounge.

After Beth left them, Cam looked at Sandy. "You want to go first?"

"You take longer," Sandy teased. "I'll watch some tv while you shower."

"Right," Cam answered, and left the room.

Sandy eased down into a recliner and turned on the television. She was surprised to see footage of their return to the command center earlier in the day with the sisters and the Martin family onboard. Sandy didn't remember seeing any news cameras. She had to laugh when she turned toward the camera, and Amite's head poked out of her shirt. She may have been oblivious to their presence, but Amite was sure to get his fifteen seconds of fame as the camera zoomed in on him. Sandy got up from her seat and knocked on the door before opening it.

"We made it on the news," she called into Cam.

"What?" Cam replied through a thick cloud of steam.

"We made it on the local news when we came in earlier with a boat full of survivors."

"I don't remember seeing a news camera. Do you?" Cam asked.

"No, but Amite had a great cameo shot." Sandy laughed. "Enjoy your shower."

Sandy returned to the recliner and was beginning to doze off when Cam entered the room. "I feel human again," she said, startling Sandy. "Did I catch you napping?"

"I dang near fell asleep waiting for you," Sandy smirked.

"There are plastic drawstring bags for your dirty clothes," Cam said as she finished brushing out her hair. "I sure didn't want to put those smelly things back in my suitcase."

"Me either. I hear that shower calling my name. Keep your eyes on the tv, and you may see that video clip." Sandy picked up her bag and entered the bathroom.

Cam settled in the comfortable chair and realized how easy it would be to fall asleep. It didn't take long before the news clip cycled back around, and she watched the video of their return to the command center. Cam chuckled and leaned back to close her eyes. The clean clothing and relaxing shower had worked magic, and she dozed while waiting for Sandy.

Sandy stripped out of her clothes and stepped into the pulsing shower. She thought she had gone to heaven when the hot water began pulsing across her back. She felt the grime from the last few days and the stress in her body melt away. *We definitely need to buy one of these showerheads.* Sandy lathered and rinsed her hair twice before it felt clean and then worked on the rest of her body. Cam had dressed in jeans, but Sandy felt like it was time to pull out some cargo shorts. The previous night had been moderately cool, so she didn't worry about getting chilled during the night. Sandy brushed her teeth and pulled her hair into a ponytail. "It feels good to be clean again," she told the image smiling back at her from the mirror. After bagging up her dirty clothes, Sandy walked into the lounge. Cam was asleep, softly snoring as she snuggled in the comfortable chair.

Sandy reached down to shake her shoulder gently. "Hey, sleepyhead. It's time to go."

"Just ten more minutes, please," Cam groaned.

"We need one of these chairs and a showerhead like that at home. That shower was heavenly."

"I will put it on our Christmas list," Cam said as she stretched and sat upright. "I don't often fall asleep like that, but it sure was comfortable."

"Are you ready to make an exit and head back over to the command center? I don't know about you, but I'm ready for a cold beer and grilled oysters."

"That does sound good." Cam stood and picked up her bags.

They said goodbye to Beth who wished them well. Beth reminded them to stop by anytime they were in the area, and Sandy assured her they would.

The sun was quickly fading as they drove back to the command center. Someone had been busy transforming the empty parking lot into a small dining area with tables and chairs, so Cam went to their parking spot where they would spend the night. She tossed an arm around Sandy as they walked toward the tent.

"I'm glad we got to do this together."

"Me too. I think it was a good experience for both of us. Do you think we could do it again?"

Cam smiled at her baby sister. "No doubt about that."

"Good. I'd like that."

†

Woody met them as they entered the tent to collect Amite. "I can't thank you ladies enough for helping us out. We wouldn't have been able to reach those families for another day or two without your assistance."

"We were delighted to help out, and we'd like to help in the future if needed," Cam said and looked at Sandy, who nodded in agreement. "Do we need to return the banner back to you?"

"No, you've earned the right to fly it, and you're officially part of the Cajun Navy now. The National Guard collected your contact information and will contact you for future events. If there is one thing you can predict about Mother Nature, it's that she's danged unpredictable." Woody chuckled at his comment. "Every year there seem to be more and more events occurring."

"That's the truth," Sandy said. "About the only time we can't volunteer is during gator season since that brings in so much of the family income for the year."

"That's understandable," Woody answered. "We wouldn't expect you to respond for every event, so just help out when you can."

"I feel like we came late to this party. When should we plan to show up next time?" Cam asked.

"Whenever it's safe to travel to the area that's affected. The last thing we need is our volunteers in danger. You ladies arrived just when we needed you most."

"Is there anything else we can do before we head home?" Sandy asked.

"Yes, enjoy one heck of a fine dinner," Woody chuckled. "With the water gone down as much as it has already today, I think the ground forces will take over tomorrow. We do appreciate everything that you two did and hope you will enjoy a good meal with us."

"We are looking forward to that," Sandy grinned. "The smell of those grilled oysters is killing me."

"Go get some. Try the hushpuppies too. They are tasty." He grinned at Sandy. "You're old enough to drink, right?"

"Yes, sir, I am," she laughed. "That will be my first stop."

"Enjoy then, and thanks again, ladies."

"Thanks, Woody." Cam shook his hand, and they went in search of Amite and some cold beer.

Reba had Amite tucked into the large breast pocket of her apron as she spread disposable tablecloths on the tables. She looked up when she saw Cam and Sandy approaching.

"You two look refreshed." She smiled.

"That shower was heavenly," Sandy said. "Has he been a good boy?"

"He's a little angel. Just tucks in and starts to purring," Reba said as she gently eased Amite from her pocket. She handed him to Sandy. "I'd be willing to keep him, but I think he's found his mama."

"I think so, too," Sandy said as she brought the kitten up and kissed his head. Amite rubbed her chin.

"A match made in heaven," Cam said. "What can we help you do?"

"Not a thing. Draw up a couple of beers and grab a seat. The oysters will start rolling out soon." She wiped her hands. "I'll bring you a basket of hushpuppies and some cheese dip to hold you over."

"Thanks, Ms. Reba." Cam looked at Sandy. "You two, find us a spot, and I'll grab some beer. Close enough where we can watch the action." Cam grinned.

Sandy took a seat at the first table, close enough to watch the cook preparing the char-grilled oysters. An older man sat beside him at a table, shucking the oysters and dropping the empty half shells into a plastic bucket. Sandy watched how easily he split the oysters in two, separating the meat from the shell, placing them on large baking pans until the cook put them on the grill, and adding a prepared topping of seasonings.

The man caught Sandy watching him and she smiled. "You look like you've done that once or twice."

"I'd be a rich man if I had a penny for every oyster I ever shucked, Little Missy," he said.

"You make it look so effortless. I've shucked before, but never as smooth as you."

"Just takes practice. Would you like a few raw while you're waiting?"

"I'd love some," Sandy replied. "Those look so delicious."

"Maybe by the time you finish these, the grilled will start coming off the cooker." He brought her over a tray of oysters.

"Now we are talking," Cam said as she arrived with two cups of beer.

"I'm right behind you, so don't stop suddenly," Ms. Reba said. "I've brought some crackers and sauces for the oysters. Lemon slices, too." She placed a tray in front of Sandy. "I saw Marcus and Sandy chatting it up, and I knew it would only be seconds before he offered her some raw." Reba chuckled.

"These are some pretty oysters," Cam said as she used a small fork to mix up some sauce. She added a squeeze of lemon, some horseradish, and a big shot of hot sauce to a bowl of cocktail sauce. "Now we can eat." Cam offered Sandy and Reba a cracker.

Sandy put the oyster on the saltine and dabbed a healthy dose of Cam's concoction across the oyster. When she popped the cracker in her mouth and started chewing, she let out a moan. When she swallowed, she looked back at Marcus.

"These are fantastic."

"I'll keep shucking as long as you keep eating. I heard about the two of y'all on the news. We need to feed you up right, so you come back; God forbid we need you again."

"We'll be here as fast as we can," Sandy promised.

"Yeah, I heard y'all made it on the news," Ms. Reba said. "Handsome boy here was an instant media sensation," she said, scratching Amite's chin. "I didn't figure his tummy was ready for seafood yet, but I did bring him some wet food. Would it be okay if I fed him?"

"That would be more than fine," Sandy said.

Ms. Reba reached down and plucked Amite from Sandy's lap. "We'll be back later."

Sandy smiled at Cam, who was going for a second oyster. "These taste so good raw I can't imagine they could taste better grilled."

Cam pointed toward the grill. "I do believe you are about to find that out."

Sandy's head spun around to find Marcus approaching with a large platter of grilled oysters.

"Be careful. These just came off the grill. Try them without sauce first, and I bet you'll find you don't need anything else. Place the oyster on a cracker or a piece of French bread toast and drizzle the butter in the shell on top. I promise you won't find any better than these."

"You haven't steered us wrong yet." Sandy smiled up at him.

"The hardest part is waiting for them to cool enough to eat," Cam said and took a drink of beer.

Boats and trucks began returning for the night. Soon after, others, mostly men, joined them and spread out among the tables after grabbing cups of beer. "How are they, ladies?" One of the men asked as he sat next to Sandy.

"Almost sinful," Sandy said and placed another grilled oyster in her mouth.

"We're Cam and Sandy from Morganza," Cam offered.

"Rich, Blue, and Ralph from Lafayette," he answered. "Welcome to the Cajun Navy."

"Thanks. It's been an enlightening experience," Sandy said. "Until now, I've taken the power and wrath of Mother Nature for granted."

"This is an excellent but disheartening way of learning that lesson. Our first adventure was Katrina. For months after, we swore we'd never get involved again, but when the next disaster hit, there was no holding us back."

"How many have you worked?" Sandy asked.

"This makes five for us. Some men that started the Cajun Navy years ago have been on many more." Rich shook his head. "I don't think we've ever eaten this good on a campaign, though, so don't expect this every time."

"This is quite a spread tonight," Cam said. The propane cooker whooshed as the flame ignited. "With more to come."

"I saw them unloading some royal red shrimp earlier, so we're in for a fantastic treat. I swear those shrimps are as sweet as a lobster." Rich smiled and took a long drink of beer. "Can I get you, ladies, a refill?"

"Thanks. That would be great," Cam said.

"Sit tight on those refills. I'm coming with a pitcher. You all keep eating." Charlotte waved an empty pitcher toward them.

Cam turned to Rich. "You heard the lady. The service around here is impeccable."

"I noticed your caps say Gator Girlz. What's that all about?"

"The two of us and our three sisters own Gator Girlz, Inc. We harvest gators, catfish, crawfish, and have a few other business ventures on the side," Sandy informed him.

Rich's eyebrows shot up. "You fish for gators? No offense, but you're no bigger than a minute."

"She can fight a gator with the best of them," Cam proudly said. "She may be small, but dynamite comes in small packages."

Sandy grinned. "Daddy taught us all how to hunt and fish as soon as we were big enough. I'm the baby and the runt, but I work just as hard as my sisters."

"Harder on some days," Cam shot her a wink. "I've never seen anyone who loves to fish as much as Sandy does. Since she was about in the sixth grade, she'd come home from school and hit the bayou to catch as many cats as she could to drop off at the processors before dark."

"It still gives me great pleasure to drop off a big load of channel cats that weigh more than me."

"That's very impressive. I've heard of a rare female gator hunter, but certainly not a whole family of them." Rich laughed softly. "I reckon you learn something every day. How many tags y'all fill every season?"

Cam looked at Sandy. "We are using two boats again this year, so we've upped our tags. We've got three hundred fifty tags to fill."

Rich let out a low whistle. "That's a lot of tags to fill in a thirty-day season."

Sandy nodded. "Lots of hard work and long days, but we've never turned a tag back in that we couldn't fill."

"You guys get much of an opportunity to hunt?" Cam asked.

"A bit of deer hunting when we can. Most of us work offshore," Rich answered.

Cam looked at him. "We have an annual hog hunt just after Christmas if you would like to join us. We've got a wild hog infestation we have to cull every year. We usually have a pig pickin, and harvest some meat for local families who need some extra meat for their freezers."

"That's a fantastic idea. I know some families in our community that could benefit from that."

Cam pulled out a business card and handed it to him. "We usually start the hunt the twenty-eighth, so we start the New Year off with a full belly."

Sandy swallowed an oyster. "Give us a call if you'd like to join in the hunt and take a few hogs back with you. It helps us somewhat control the growth of the population, and gives food to people that may not have much."

"I bet them hogs are as bad as rabbits," Rich teased.

"They breed constantly, so we have to thin them regularly on the island." Cam wiped her mouth. "I do believe we have more oysters on the way."

"Man, these things are addicting," Sandy said.

They continued to feast on the grilled oysters until large platters were brought to them mounded with shrimp-boil items.

"Holy cow, that's a lot of food." Sandy's eyes grew wide as she looked at the portion set in front of her.

"Let me know if you need help, little sister," Rich teased. He pulled off several paper towels and handed the roll to Sandy. "Let's do this."

An hour later, neither Cam nor Sandy had made it to the bottom of the platter.

"I swear I'm gonna die if I eat another bite," Sandy groaned.

"I guess you didn't save room for bread pudding with bourbon sauce then," Charlotte said.

"Aw hell, naw," Sandy said. "Can I get a container to go, though, for later?"

"Of course, you can. I'll bring you two over."

"Thanks, Charlotte. That was one fine meal. I can't remember the last time we ate this good," Sandy told her.

Cam smiled at Rich. "Good company, too. It was a pleasure meeting you. I think it's time for us to head off for now. We're starting for home tomorrow early."

"The pleasure was all mine. I look forward to hunting with you at the end of the year, so I'll see you then, if not sooner." He shrugged. "Hopefully, no disasters arrive the rest of the year."

"If they do, we'll be right there with you if we can," Sandy promised and shook his hand.

"Travel safe, and thanks again for joining us. You're much better looking than the rest of this lot," Rich teased.

Charlotte brought them containers filled with bread pudding. "I can't thank you enough for everything you all have done. What time will you be heading out in the morning?"

"By six at the latest," Cam replied.

"Good, I can fill your bellies up once more for the road. Biscuits and gravy sound good to you?"

"Perfect, Charlotte," Sandy answered. "We'll see you in the morning."

"Goodnight, ladies. Rest well."

"I have got to get rid of some beer," Cam said as they walked toward the truck.

"Me too," Sandy chuckled. "I think my teeth were beginning to float."

†

When they returned to the truck, they climbed onto the bed and stretched out on the air mattress.

"It's turned into such a beautiful night," Sandy said as she petted Amite, who was curled in her lap.

Cam placed an arm around Sandy's shoulder. "When we get home, it's back to business as usual, but I wanted to thank you for all you've done. It's always great working alongside you, but I think we both grew a bit this trip. We can't take life for granted. We work hard, but I think we both need to get out and live a bit more too."

"I agree, and I think it's time you ramp things up a bit with that sexy deputy of yours."

"That will be my number one personal goal for this year. I think we've got a shot at something special."

"Tab worthy?"

"Nobody will ever replace Tab in my heart, but I know there's room for another special love, and I think Luce is the one."

"That makes me warm all over to hear you talk like that. Liz has been hinting at a few nurses at the hospital that may prove interesting. Maybe I'll dip my toes in the dating pool too."

"Maybe we can double date. Unless I'll cramp your style."

"If I only had a style to cramp," Sandy chuckled.

"You may think I'm nuts, which I probably am, but that bread pudding is calling my name," Cam said. "Can you reach it through the back window?"

"It just so happens I left it in a very convenient spot," Sandy replied. "Hold Amite for a second, and I'll grab it."

"Let him sleep. I'll get it." Cam turned around and located the two containers of bread pudding and spoons Charlotte had given them. She handed one to Sandy and settled in beside her. She scooped a spoonful. "Here's to a beautiful night under the stars spent with my best friend." Cam tapped spoons with Sandy and noticed her eyes were shining.

"Am I really your best friend, Cam?"

"Always have been, always will be," Cam replied.

"Good to know," Sandy answered and took a bite of the delicious dessert. "Oh, my lord. I think I'm gonna die cause I'm gonna eat every last bite."

"Me too."

Cam tossed the empty containers into a small garbage bag and stretched out beside Sandy. "I think I will sleep like a baby tonight. Goodnight, Squirt."

"Goodnight, Cam."

Sandy gazed up at the beautiful clear sky and watched as a jet streaked overhead.. The moon had risen, and a faint ring glowed around it. Sandy listed to the chorus of crickets along the highway, and when she was about to doze off, she saw a shooting star blaze through the darkness. She turned to Cam to ask if she had seen it, but Cam was already fast asleep. *I guess that treasure was all mine.* Sandy pulled a light blanket over her body and snuggled into Amite, who was purring in delight as he chased his prey in his dreams. "Goodnight, sweet boy."

CHAPTER SIX

Sandy woke the next morning to the sounds of traffic on the highway. Interstate 12 had reopened, and the large trucks were bumper to bumper. That was a good sign that goods were on the move again, but her dream was disturbed. Sandy couldn't quite remember the details, but she remembered it was pleasant. She laughed when a trucker hit his air brakes, and Cam sat straight up on the mattress.

"Not the greatest alarm clock, is it?"

"Holy shit, I didn't know what was happening. Good morning, Squirt."

"Let's get packed up and get some breakfast before hitting the road." Sandy picked up Amite and climbed out of the truck.

"I'll roll up our sleeping bags if you want to tend to the little one," Cam offered.

"Thanks. I'll deflate the air mattress if you release the valve while I feed Amite."

The sisters busied themselves, storing the equipment they had used and getting ready for the trip home. Charlotte saw them approach as they drove toward the tent and had two large portions of biscuit and gravy prepared for them while Reba poured juice and coffee.

"I bet you're excited to get back home," Reba said as she set the drinks in front of them.

"Yes, but this has been a great experience. Cam says it's going to take us days to work off all this great food," Sandy teased.

Reba shook her head. "I don't believe that for a minute as hard as the two of you work. I'm glad I got to meet y'all."

"I wish it had been under better circumstances," Sandy replied.

"Me, too, but we have to take what fate designs for us," Reba answered. "Can I get you two anything else? Something for the road, maybe?"

Sandy shook her head. "If we eat all of this, it will hold us until we get home. I may be so full I have to take a nap."

"I was thinking the same thing," Cam chuckled. "Better make it a coffee to go, then."

"I'll have one ready for you when you finish eating. Just holler if you need anything else."

"Thanks, Ms. Reba." Sandy took another bite. "If you stayed here a few more days, you might put some of your weight back on."

"No doubt, but I'm ready to be home."

"Me too." Sandy dipped a finger into the gravy and offered it to Amite. He eagerly licked her finger. "I reckon I better be careful. It's a long ride home, and I don't want his tummy upset."

"Uh-hm, I was thinking the same thing." Cam took a sip of apple juice. "You know, I thought we should try some apple pie shine this year. I bet it would be tasty."

"That does sound good. I bet it would be a big hit too. We can check on some apples when we get home or hit a Farmer's Market somewhere. How do you plan to share the news with Luce?"

Cam's forehead wrinkled. "I haven't figured that out yet. That may be a major stumbling block for us."

"I sure hope not. Luce is good for you. I'd hate for something like that to come between you. I know it's illegal but her boss, Scott, is one of our best customers."

"I'll find a way to cross that bridge once we determine if we're going to be serious about a relationship."

When they finished their meals, Cam and Sandy dumped their trash and hugged Charlotte and Ms. Reba. "Thank you for taking such good care of us," Sandy said.

"It was a pleasure. Reba has your coffee, and I packed a few biscuits for the ride, just in case you get hungry," Charlotte said, handing a bag to Sandy.

"Travel safe, my angels," Reba said with tears in her eyes. She hugged each of them and smiled. "Take good care of each other and your family."

"We will," Sandy replied and nodded to Cam. "We better go before the tears start to fall."

As they walked to the truck, Cam turned to wave a final goodbye, then climbed behind the wheel. "Let's go home."

†

Sandy reclined the seat, and Amite curled up on her stomach. Cam looked over at them. "He sure is a cutie."

"Lovable little rascal, too. I reckon I need to get a vet appointment for him to get him checked out." Sandy stroked down his side.

"He looks pretty healthy, but he probably needs deworming and started on his shots. Do you want to call and see if we can get an appointment this afternoon?"

"Might as well get him started right." Sandy pulled out the phone and made an appointment for one o'clock. "All set."

"It looks like most of the traffic is heading into Baton Rouge, and we beat the traffic coming out," Cam said as she saw the line of semi-trucks crawling along the Interstate. "I sure am glad we are heading this way."

Sandy nodded in agreement. "It will be good to be home. I hope Wanda has a hot meal cooked. I'm getting used to all this good eating."

"Last night's meal was incredible. I think it would make the drive worthwhile to come down and eat at their restaurant. Maybe we can plan a day trip on Luce's day off soon."

"Now that's a great idea. Maybe make it an overnight stay?"

"Hmm, I wonder if I could get a pair of tickets to a football game."

"Ask Coach. I'm sure she could get you some. That woman adores you."

"What's not to love?" Cam chuckled. "Hey, look." Cam pointed to a road sign advertising a Farmer's Market. "Wanna check it out?"

"Why not. We've got time before Amite's appointment." Sandy raised her seat. "Maybe we'll find a good deal on some apples or other produce."

"Only one way to find out." Cam turned on her blinker and took the exit.

There were not many vehicles when they entered the parking lot, and Cam looked at the clock on her dash. "We might be a bit early, but let's take a look."

Sandy tucked Amite inside her shirt as they exited the truck and began walking toward the building full of vendor stalls. The aroma of fresh baked goods filled the air. Sandy looked at Cam. "There is no way we can be hungry after that breakfast, but damn something sure smells good."

"You two go track down the baked goods, and I'll start down the produce aisle."

"Sure thing, Cam," Sandy said and went in search of the delicious scent wafting in the air.

Cam watched them go with a smile. Sure, Sandy was grown, but there would always be a bit of little girl in her spirit. "Let me see what I can find." She hit the jackpot when she saw a farmer backing his truck into a stall loaded with half dozen bushels of apples and pears. She waited for him to exit the vehicle and was surprised when a woman emerged from behind the wheel.

"Good morning," Cam offered.

"Well, a good morning to you," the woman beamed a bright smile at Cam.

"Is that your load for the day?" Cam asked.

"Yes, it'll be the last of the fruits with all this danged rain," the woman said.

"How much, for all of it?"

The woman did a double take. She wasn't sure she had heard Cam right. "How much do you want?"

"If my math is correct, you have six bushels of apples and six bushels of pears. Would you like to save us both some extra work and just load it into my truck?"

"I normally get fifteen a bushel, but if you want them all, I can cut you a deal and go home early today," the woman answered.

"I'll pay your price. We all have a living to make." Cam pulled out two one-hundred-dollar bills and handed them to the woman.

"I'll be right back with your change," she said and hurried back to her truck.

Cam waited patiently and scoured the nearby stalls. When the woman handed her the change, Cam asked, "Who would have some nice melons? I'm looking for watermelon, honeydew, and cantaloupes if possible."

"Your best bet would be Mr. Paul. He should have all of those. He usually sets up at the last stall on the left. C'mon, I'll introduce you and see if he has what you need. Then I can load your fruit into your vehicle."

Cam followed her until they reached the end of the row of stalls. A weathered older man sat on a stool, peeling an apple. "Mornin', ladies."

"Hey, Mr. Paul, this woman would like to buy some of your melons," she said.

"Well, I reckon she came to the right spot." He looked closely at Cam. "I seen you on tv, didn't I?"

"Yes, sir, you might have. My sister and I have been helping out with rescues down in the Baton Rouge area."

"With a cute little black cat." He grinned at her, revealing several missing teeth.

"That would be Amite. My baby sister, Sandy, rescued him from becoming gator bait," Cam replied.

Right on cue, Sandy and Amite arrived. She was holding a bag of fresh-baked apple turnovers.

"Let me guess. Fresh apple turnovers from Mary T?" Mr. Paul said.

"Yes, sir, it was the first thing I smelled when we got here. I had to track down what smelled so good."

"They are delicious. Hey there, little one," Mr. Paul spoke softly to Amite. Then he turned back to Cam. "What you looking for?"

"Watermelons, honeydews, and cantaloupes if you have them," she answered.

"I got everything but the cantaloupes."

Cam turned to Sandy and handed her the truck keys. "Will you bring the truck around so we can load the apples and pears into the airboat while Mr. Paul and I do some negotiating?"

Sandy smiled. "Sure thing, Cam."

"I got some big ole watermelons this year. Sweet as they can be. I get eight dollars each for 'em. How many are you looking to buy?"

"A dozen of your biggest, and three dozen honeydews if ya got 'em?" Cam said.

"I got 'em, but what ya gonna do with all this fruit?" he grinned.

"I've got a big family waiting on us at home," Cam replied with a wink.

"Gotcha," Mr. Paul said. "Makes no difference to me what ya do with it. I was just curious."

"No problem," Cam replied, grinning. "What's my total?"

"A hundred eighty-six," Mr. Paul said.

Cam pulled out her wallet and handed him two one-hundred-dollar bills. "Keep the change if you help me load them."

"Let me get a bale of straw to bed them in if that's okay. It'll keep 'em from rolling around if you puttin' 'em in an airboat."

"If you want to drive around first, we can load up your apples and pears first, and then y'all can put the melons in the middle."

"That's a great idea. We'll be back in a few minutes, Mr. Paul. Meet you back at your stall?"

"That works for me. We'll get you loaded and back for your melons so you can get on the road."

"Thanks," Cam said. She walked over to the truck and climbed in. "Pull around back first. We're going to load the apples and pears first, then come back for melons. You okay putting this in the airboat? Mr. Paul has a bale of straw he's gonna give us."

"Might as well. We can take the goodies straight to the island and set up the mash while we're cooking tonight."

"Great minds think alike," Cam smirked.

When they pulled to the back of the stalls, the woman, whose name was Carol, had pulled her truck around to make it easier for them to load.

Cam smiled. "Did the charge cover the cost of the baskets?"

"Normally, no, but since you bought me out today, I can toss in the baskets. I get them relatively cheap."

"Will twenty cover them?" Sandy asked.

"Yes, but really, it's not necessary," Carol said.

"Please?" Sandy said. "We all have expenses to cover these days."

Carol tucked the twenty in her pocket, and she and Cam began carrying the bushel baskets to Sandy in the bed of the boat. When they had finished, Carol told them, "I'll follow you to Mr. Paul's and help load. These baskets were the easy stuff."

"Much appreciated," Cam said. "Let's go."

Mr. Paul told Sandy how to spread the straw around to cushion the melons. "As long as you don't go off-roading, I think you'll be fine."

"No plans for that," Sandy said as she took the first melon Cam handed her.

Mr. Paul had been busy sorting out the melons, picking the largest he had per Cam's request. Cam noticed there were four extra melons and six extra honeydews. "Mr. Paul, I know your math is good, but there are extras in there."

"A thank you for all you two did for them folks that got flooded out," he grinned.

"Well, we thank you, sir, for your kindness." Cam shook his hand. "You here on the weekends?"

"Until the crops stop producing. Why?"

"I may drop in on you some weekend with a surprise." Cam winked.

"You'd be more than welcome." Mr. Paul grinned back at her.

"We'll see you soon. Let's hit the road, Squirt."

†

They made good time on the Interstate, and when they reached the turn for their state road, Cam let out a whoop. "Almost home."

Sandy looked at the GPS. "We should hit town just in time to drop the trailer."

"Naw, we'll go ahead and take Amite to his appointment. Then we can launch the boat and unload the truck. Maybe by then, Wanda will have something for dinner, and we can go over to the island later to cook."

†

Amite was not a happy camper when they left the vet's office. The shots were terrible enough, but when they violated him to check his temperature, he'd had his fill, and the hissing, growling, and scratching began. Sandy cradled him in her arms, and once they were back in the truck, he settled down.

Sandy was glad to see the driveway to their home. "You're home for good now, baby boy," she told him and kissed his head. "Go ahead and drive down to the boat ramp, and I'll take the boat off. You can drop the trailer while I tie off the boat."

"Sounds like a plan. It shouldn't take long to unload the truck," Cam said as she backed down the boat ramp. "Should we just dump everything at my place? I might stay out on the island tonight."

"Do you want some company?"

"Silly question. I've been snuggled up with you on an air mattress for a couple of nights. Of course, I'd love for you to stay."

Willow raced out of the house when Wanda opened the door. She rushed toward Sandy, who carefully tucked Amite back in her shirt.

Willow, a Catahoula pup, had been a Christmas gift from Tab to Cam, but when Cam returned to school for a final year, Willow and Sandy had become inseparable. In the beginning, it was tough to gauge which of them missed Cam more.

"Hey, my girl," Sandy said as she knelt next to Willow. "Did you miss us?"

Willow covered her face with kisses in response. "I've got a baby brother I want you to meet," Sandy softly spoke to the dog. "He's little and needs a big sister. Sit."

Willow's rear end wiggled with excitement, but she followed Sandy's command and dropped to her haunches. Sandy eased Amite from her shirt, petting his head as Willow whined. She slowly stepped forward, smelling the kitten, and then licked his head. Amite wasn't scared and reached out his paws with his claws retracted and hugged Willow's muzzle.

"Aw, that's sweet, you two," Sandy said, stroking down Willow's head. Sandy looked up at Cam. "Can they go with us tonight?"

"Heck yeah. I think Amite and Willow need some supervised time to bond, and there's no time like the present to get them started on the right foot." Cam's hand patted Willow's back. "That's a good girl."

Wanda walked over to them and hugged each one of them. "It's great to have you home." She took a look at the haul of fruit in the airboat. "It looks like we'll be busy for a while."

"We stopped off at a Farmer's Market on our way home," Cam explained, but Wanda wasn't listening. She was reaching for Amite.

"So, this is the cutie you told me about?" Wanda asked Sandy.

"Yep, he's a real charmer," Sandy replied as she relinquished Amite to Wanda. He immediately started purring as she held him close.

"I can see and hear that," Wanda replied. "What's the plan for tonight?"

Cam was the first to speak. "We're going to unpack the truck, maybe grab something to eat and then head out to the island to unload and start making some mash while we cook."

"Well, you're in luck on both accounts. T and I took out the mash we have ready to cook this morning. We figured you'd jump right back into cooking since we've gotten so many calls." She smiled at Sandy. "I've got baby-back ribs and sweet potatoes in the oven for supper."

"Oh, heck yes," Sandy replied.

"If you two want to unpack and head out to the island, I'll bring out supper when it gets ready. Liz should be home from her shift soon, so I'll load some sugar and yeast in the boat. There should be plenty of empty barrels at the cook shack for the new mash. We'll come over and have supper with you, then help with the fruit for a bit."

"That would be wonderful. As soon as darkness falls, we'll crank up the still and get to cooking." Sandy was grinning from ear to ear.

Cam was dropping the trailer from the truck. Wanda asked. "Do y'all need help unpacking?"

"Naw, we're going to stay out on the island tonight, so we're just going to dump everything at my place," Cam answered.

"I'll see you later then. Do you need something to snack on until dinner?"

"Thanks, Wanda, but we've still got biscuits and some apple turnovers we can eat to hold us over," Sandy replied.

"Dang, I had forgotten about those." Cam walked around to climb into the truck, then pulled it next to her front porch.

Wanda looked at Sandy. "She doing okay?"

"Yes, she's the Great Cam St. Angelo," Sandy teased. "She saw some heartbreaking things down south, but she's okay. Ready to get back to work. You know how Cam is."

Cam had climbed the steps and opened her front door. "Let's go, Squirt," she called to Sandy.

"See what I mean?" Sandy laughed.

"You want me to keep Amite with me?"

"Nope, he and Willow are going out to the island with us," Sandy said. "I'll come to grab him before the ride over if you want to spend a few minutes with him while we unpack."

"Deal. You better run before the boss gets impatient." Wanda chuckled.

"See ya, Wanda." Sandy jogged over to the truck and began tossing bags and equipment to where Cam was waiting on the porch as Wanda and the animals returned inside.

†

Cam waited at the dock while Sandy retrieved Amite and Willow for the ride to the island. She gazed across the

116

peaceful water, watching the herons wading along the shore to catch minnows for a meal. The rumbling sound of traffic brought her attention to the yellow school bus that would be slowing to a stop at the end of their drive in a few seconds to drop Karen's boys off from school. Cam knew Karen would be feeding them snacks and loading them up for football practice at six when the sun started to fade and the temps dropped a few degrees. Life at the homestead was back to normal. The activity was buzzing everywhere, and that's how they lived. She watched Sandy approach and bent to untie the airboat from the dock. Willow jumped onto the boat and carefully picked a spot to sit while Sandy and Amite took the driver's seat.

"All set?" Cam asked before stepping onboard.

"Yep, let's do this," Sandy said and turned the ignition.

Cam nodded, coiled up the rope, and took her seat beside Sandy. It took minutes for Sandy to drive across the bayou to the island where the family hunted, cooked shine, and fished. Cam had beautiful memories of the island and often spent time in the small cabin she thought of as her second home. Sandy spun the airboat around, and Cam stepped off to secure the mooring line.

"Why don't you put Amite and Willow in the cabin until we finish unloading. I wouldn't want him to get into any trouble unsupervised."

"Not a bad idea," Sandy agreed and called Willow from the boat.

Cam began unloading the bushels of apples and pears, placing them on the dock while Sandy secured the animals. "Let's carry these in, and you can help me get some mash cooking, then we'll finish unloading."

"I'll help you pour the mash, and while you get the still up and running, I'll continue to unload. I think I can use a tub to put the honeydews in and carry them that way."

"Or you could pull a Gator around with a trailer and let it do the hard work," Cam suggested.

"Good thing you're older and wiser."

"I come in handy sometimes," Cam smirked. "Let's carry a bushel, and then you can help me pour the mash in the vat. After that, you can use the Gator."

Sandy and Cam poured the first barrel of mash into the vat. Cam added the cold water, started the flame, and began pasting the lid's seal to prevent moisture and pressure from escaping. Cam heard the Gator motor revving and knew Sandy was on the way to the dock. Pasting the seal was a slow, painstaking job, but one crucial to the safe and efficient operation of the still. Cam knew she couldn't rush this process.

Sandy pulled the trailer close to the dock and loaded several bushels of fruit. She went ahead and loaded the watermelons and honeydew melons on the pier. Sandy would grab a container for them on her first run to the shack. It was full dark now, and she could hear the calls of bull gators in the distance. One bellow was much deeper than the rest, and Sandy recognized Bubba Gump, a monstrously colossal gator known as the demon of the swamp. Sandy had dreamed for years that she would be the hunter to finally catch him and collect the bounty placed on his head.

"One day, big boy," she said and climbed onto the vehicle.

When she pulled to a stop in front of the shack, Cam turned toward her. "Keep pasting. I've got this." Cam turned around and resumed her work.

Sandy unloaded the bushels and grabbed a plastic tub for the honeydews before heading back to the dock.

Sandy was on her third load when she looked up to see the light from Wanda's boat cutting through the darkness. Cam walked up to help her transport the fruit. "The cavalry has arrived."

"I hope the cavalry has dinner. I'm suddenly hungry. That apple turnover is long gone."

Sandy smiled back at Cam. "Mine is too. My mouth has been watering ever since Wanda mentioned ribs."

"Let's see how much we can get moved before they arrive, and then we can take a meal break."

"Just a few more trips and we will have it licked." Sandy tossed a watermelon to Cam to load. "Damn, these things are heavy."

"They will make some beautiful Red Bliss," Cam replied. "I would like to take a gallon to Mr. Paul and maybe some apple pie to Carol."

"That sounds like a relaxing Sunday morning drive. But not this Sunday." Sandy grinned.

They emptied the load and worked on a second before Liz and Wanda pulled up at the dock. The motion sensor lights came on to light up the pier.

"Hey, strangers," Liz said as she stepped off the boat and waited for Wanda to hand her a box of food.

"Hey, there, yourself," Sandy called back. "Do you need a hand?"

"Nope, I think we've got it, but you can run ahead and open the door."

"Hey, Squirt, don't forget the fur babies are in there. I don't want them tripping anyone," Cam warned.

"Got it." Sandy jogged ahead and scooped up Amite when she opened the door.

"What a cutie," Liz said when she came through the door.

"You should hear the purr box on that little boy. He rumbles like a mini-version of Bubba Gump," Wanda teased.

"I pray he doesn't grow up to be just as mean then," Liz said as she placed the box of food on the table. "Wanda and I will get things set up in here if you'll get Cam inside. We can all pitch in after we eat. Trust me, we'll need a workout to burn these calories."

"I plan to work a bunch off of you later. These two are staying out here tonight, so you can get as loud as you want." Wanda chuckled.

"Dear Lord." Sandy shook her head and placed Amite on the floor before leaving to assist Cam. She walked back to the dock just as Cam loaded the last watermelon. "Boss Wanda says to come in, and we'll all pitch in to finish unloading after dinner."

"Fine with me," Cam said, wiping the sweat from her brow. "Those are some damn fine watermelons. You go ahead. I'm gonna check the temperature, and I'll be right behind you."

"Please don't make her send me out again. You know how grumpy she can get."

"Go, I'll be a minute or two behind you," Cam replied and shooed Sandy away.

Sandy turned toward the cabin, and Cam entered the shack. She could hear the vat boiling and looked down to check the temp. "Coming right along."

Cam studied the seal on the lid and, satisfied the cook was going well, headed for the cabin.

Wanda was pouring the tea when Cam entered. "Perfect timing."

"Damn, it smells good in here," Cam said as she walked to the sink to wash her hands.

"Wait until you see these ribs," Sandy replied. "Huge and meaty."

"She's been dreaming of your ribs ever since you mentioned them," Cam said, and ruffled Sandy's hair as she walked by her.

"Nothing wrong with that. Take a seat, and let's get to eating," Liz said.

Cam split open a sweet potato and covered it with butter, then took a portion of ribs for her plate. "This looks so good, Wanda. Thanks for cooking extras."

"My pleasure. I love to see how you attack my cooking." Wanda chuckled.

It was hilarious how Willow and Amite sat beside Sandy, hoping to be noticed and offered a handout. "Willow, I can see you will be a bad influence for Amite," Sandy said, but she still gave them both a small portion of meat, and Willow got a bone. "That's all you get."

"Aww, mama," Wanda said. "There's plenty for everyone."

"Yes, but I don't want stomachs torn up all night long. Amite got shots today too, so I don't want to press my luck."

Cam shot a wink to Wanda. "Just think of all those stinky puppy farts that are going to be in Sandy's room tonight. Better open a window, Squirt."

"That looks like quite a haul of fruit and melons," Liz told Cam.

"We found a friendly Farmer's Market this morning. We figured we'd got some cooking to get done to catch up on some of the orders Wanda has been taking." Cam looked at Wanda. "The melons are enormous, and I want to figure out a recipe for an apple pie brew."

"I'll see what I can dig up on the Internet. I would imagine substituting some of the cane sugar with brown sugar, for starters," Wanda said. "Some cinnamon and nutmeg too."

"It'll be a few days before the mash is ready, so we have time," Cam replied.

"Maybe we should run a few small batches to experiment until we get the mix down," Sandy said.

"Good idea. I can't wait to try the honeydew," Liz said.

"After we finish unloading, do you want some help slicing the fruit and melons for mash?" Wanda waited for Cam to answer.

"If you have time. We will never turn down an offer of help." Cam smiled at her sister.

"I'll clean up here while y'all finish unloading. What kind of knives and equipment do we need?" Wanda asked.

"We can set up a table for all of us to work. Sandy and I both have our knives, so maybe a large butcher knife and a couple of scoops for the melons," Cam suggested. "Hey, I think we have an apple core remover, too. That would speed things up a bit."

"After a couple of hours, we can break for some coffee and cake," Wanda said. She looked at Sandy. "I made your favorite."

"You made a caramel cake?" Sandy squealed.

"Mama's recipe?" Cam asked.

"Absolutely. Everything from scratch, just like Mama made it," Wanda said.

"I'm not sure I can wait a few hours then," Cam said. "I'll try though."

Liz was the first to stand from the table. "Let's get a move on then so we can have cake."

†

Two more loads had everything stored in the shack. Cam checked the temperature and placed a quart jar underneath the drain where the liquid would arrive once it finished the process. "Shouldn't be much longer until we start getting the head from this batch," Cam announced.

"Do I need to go start a fire?" Sandy asked. They usually poured the head, the first few ounces on the fire, to test the shine. Removing this portion from the batch helped judge the proof. After they pulled off the head, it would be safe to try a taste of the shine.

"Naw, I think we'll be good. That Swamp Juice always starts strong," Cam replied. "What else did you mash in?"

"A dozen watermelons," Wanda said. "They weren't near as big or heavy as these, though. You may get two or three batches from these monsters." She placed a large melon on a tray to capture any escaping juice and sliced it open. The deep red meat of the melon glistened with juice under the light of the shack. "Man, these are pretty." She handed Liz a scoop. "Get to scooping. I'll drag a barrel over."

"Do we worry about the seeds?" Liz asked.

"Naw, they will separate, and we can strain them out before we cook," Sandy informed her. "Some folks don't even worry about them at all."

A few minutes later, Sandy turned at the sound of trickling liquid. "Here comes the head."

123

Cam nodded. "Give it a few and then dump it out and put one of the buckets underneath the flow. We can test it and see if we need to proof it down some." Cam continued coring apples before slicing them into smaller sections. Sandy was working on the pears.

"We are running low on five-gallon buckets, and we're going to need more gallon jars before the next run," Sandy said.

"Buster and Jeff got you covered. They'll be home tomorrow night and will have their truck bed loaded down," Wanda said.

"That's great news," Cam said. "We should be able to cook this batch tonight and maybe a couple of the Bliss tomorrow night while we wait on the new mash for distilling. We can make a delivery run Friday or Saturday to fill our biggest orders."

It was after eleven before they had all the fruit and melons cut for the mash. When Sandy noticed the time, she looked at Liz. "Don't you have to work in the morning?"

"Yes, I do. I know we should probably be going home. It's been good to spend time with you tonight. I think I missed y'all," Liz said as she stood and stretched.

"We missed home too. It felt so good to pull into the driveway today," Sandy replied. "A short trip is fine, but it's good to be home."

The second five-gallon bucket was nearly complete. Cam rose to change it out.

"Sit tight, big sis, I've got this," Sandy told Cam.

Wanda stood beside Liz. "Y'all don't stay up too late tonight. You've had a busy week, so try to get some rest."

"We will, as soon as this run is over," Sandy promised.

"We can add the sugar and yeast to the mash and seal it while we wait on the last buckets of this run." Cam stood and stretched. "Hey, what do you think of some strawberry and pineapple?"

"A delicious combination, but wouldn't it be expensive to make?" Sandy asked.

Cam nodded. "Yes, but I think once they got a taste, they would be willing to pay the extra price. Why don't we try a small batch for personal consumption and send out a few pints to our best customers and get their opinions?"

"I'll hit the store in the morning and buy the pineapples, strawberries, and a couple of cases of pint jars," Wanda replied.

"Thanks. If you can't find fresh pineapple, or it's crazy expensive, buy a dozen of the large cans of pineapple juice. If you can get both, we'll try it both ways."

Sandy grinned. "I do love the way you think, Cam."

"Good, you can come up with a name then, Squirt," Cam challenged her baby sister.

"No problem. Just give me a night to sleep on it."

Cam turned back to Liz and Wanda. "Thanks for dinner and all your help tonight."

"You're welcome. It was fun being out here tonight. Maybe once in a while, Liz and I can hit the crow's nest, just to make sure we don't have unexpected visitors."

Sandy nodded. "We should probably be more vigilant with more traffic on the water, especially on the weekends."

"Speaking of weekends, is Luce still coming out Sunday?" Liz asked.

"Yes, she is. She wants to meet everyone and get the grand tour."

"Do you want to stick with lasagna or do a boil since the guys will be home?"

"I'd love to have some lasagna, but a boil would be easier all around. Jeff and Buster love doing them. Maybe fry up some catfish and hushpuppies too?"

"And some boudin rolls?" Sandy tossed in.

"Yeah, we can do some of those, too," Cam laughed.

"Are you off Sunday, Liz?" Sandy asked.

"Yes, ma'am. I've got the whole weekend off."

"If T and Wanda will make the rolls, I'll catch some fresh catfish and filet them. Cam and I can do the frying if the boys will do the boil."

Liz looked at Wanda. "We can do some slaw and desserts."

"Damn, is it Sunday yet?" Sandy rubbed her hands together.

"It'll be here soon enough. We'll see you two tomorrow," Wanda said as she reached for Liz's hand. "I'll coordinate with T and Karen tomorrow."

"Be safe. We'll check out the crawfish traps in the morning before we head home. We should have a good batch by now," Sandy told them.

"Goodnight, ladies," Cam said, and swapped out buckets.

†

Cam dumped the final contents into the mash while Sandy began the cleanup from the processing. She and Cam kicked back in a chair to watch the final bucket filling.

"That was a good run. Should we take a sip to make sure of the taste?"

"Go ahead and draw us up a bit," Cam replied. "We can't skimp on quality control."

Sandy dipped a test tube into a cooling bucket and took a sip before offering it to Cam. "I do believe that's as right as it gets."

Cam swallowed. "I think you're right on, Squirt."

"Proofing it down a bit filled three of these five-gallon buckets. Do you want to use some gallon jugs for the leftover?"

"Might as well. I know we've got some locals ready for a sip or two," Cam replied. "The boys may need some to take back offshore, too."

"I do like your idea about the pineapple and strawberry. The Red Bliss does so well. The ladies seem to like a bit sweeter taste."

"It's worth a shot. It never hurts to expand your product line. Keeps the market fresh and thirsty for more."

When Sandy twisted the cap on the fourth gallon jug, she looked at Cam. "That bed is going to feel good tonight."

"That it is, Squirt. The next few days will be busy, so we better sleep while we can." She nodded toward Willow and Amite. "Those two have the right idea."

"Amite curled up with Willow two hours ago, and neither one has moved since. I hate to wake them, but it's time to hit the hay."

"You get the fur babies, and I'll lock up," Cam said. Cam's phone pinged, and she smiled when she saw it was Luce. "I'll be inside in a few."

Cam quickly punched in Luce's number. "Hey, there," she said when Luce answered.

"Hey, I'm about to get off shift, but I wanted to make sure you and Sandy made it home."

"Yes, sorry. I should have called you earlier, but we hit the ground running when we got home. I hope you like a crawfish boil because our plans changed tonight. Wanda still promises you lasagna, but the boys are home this weekend, and a boil is much easier to feed this crowd. We'll keep the lasagna down to us ladies."

"I haven't had a decent boil in a long time. That sounds perfect."

"The boys will do the boil. Sandy will catch and filet some catfish, and I'll make hushpuppies and boudin rolls. Wanda and Liz will do some sides and desserts."

"What can I do?"

"You can keep me entertained while I cook," Cam informed her. "I may need you to grab stuff for me, but otherwise, just relax and have a good time."

"I look forward to that. It's good to hear your voice."

"I missed you. Can we get together for lunch on Saturday?" Cam asked. "My treat this time."

"You have a deal. Burger Shack, okay?" Luce asked.

"That does sound good. What time?"

"Early, say eleven so you can get everything you need to do for Sunday."

"Perfect. Do you want to call tomorrow if you have time? We'll just be working around here. Checking crawfish traps and such."

"Sure, I'll give you a call before I start my shift tomorrow afternoon."

"Sounds great, Luce."

"I'll talk to you then. Goodnight, Cam."

"Goodnight. Drive safe."

CHAPTER SEVEN

The rest of the week passed quickly, and when Sunday arrived, Cam seemed a bit nervous about Luce coming to the homestead.

Sandy joined Cam at the dock, where she was pacing back and forth. "You seem a bit prickly this morning. Is everything okay?"

"I'm a bit nervous about Luce coming out. I don't want anyone to slip up and say anything about the shine."

"The family knows full well that she's a deputy, and they know better than to speak of the shack outside of our circle. Relax, and have a great day with her on the water. Then give her a ride on the island. This time of year, you'll probably see plenty of wildlife. Take some corn out and fill up the deer feeder."

Cam turned when she heard a vehicle pull up the drive.

"Take a deep breath. I'll catch our fish and have everything ready to cook by mid-afternoon." Sandy grinned. "Take the airboat. Sexy Deputy will probably love that."

Cam turned and punched Sandy playfully in the shoulder. "Thanks, Squirt. I needed a pep talk. Dad was usually the one to give it to me."

"Well, I'm glad I could be here for you. That's what best friends do. Just don't wreck my airboat."

Cam chuckled. "That would not be a great way to end a date."

"Go get her, tiger." Sandy began walking toward the house. Willow and Amite rushed to her, then turned around to look at the arriving visitor.

"Hey," Luce said when she climbed out of her car. "I hope I'm not too early."

"Heck no, we've been up for hours."

"Hey, Sandy. Is this the new addition?"

"Yes, it is, Luce. This critter is Amite, one branch away from gator bait, and this hot mess dancing around you for attention is Willow."

Willow coated Luce's cheek with kisses, causing her to laugh.

"That's amazing. It usually takes a while for Willow to warm up to strangers," Sandy said.

"Either she tastes good, or Willow just has a scent for good people," Cam replied.

"I promise I did take a shower," Luce replied. "It's good to see you again, Sandy. It sounds like y'all had a good trip."

"We did, but it's great to be home. Gator season starts in a week, so we're trying to get caught up on other chores before then. It'll be sunrise to sunset for thirty days once the season begins."

"That sounds like a lot of hard work. Maybe I could go out with you one day. I don't know how much help I could be, but maybe I could do something."

"I'd like that," Cam replied.

"We can certainly use an extra pair of hands. We've got a lot of tags to fill this year."

"How many?"

"Three hundred fifty this year," Cam answered.

"Wow, in thirty days?"

"We can easily average ten a day as long as the weather holds," Sandy said. "Especially running two boats."

"You two in one and who's in the other?"

"Wanda and T. Karen and Buster have kids, so she volunteers to cook supper for everyone, so we have a hot meal to drag home to." Sandy stroked Amite's head. "She's going to have to kittysit this year too."

"Maybe on the days I work the day shift, I can come help or cook a meal or two for y'all," Luce offered.

Cam looked at her with a puzzled expression.

"Are you surprised I can find my way around a kitchen?" Luce asked.

"Told ya so," Sandy snickered.

"Hush, Squirt," Cam warned.

Luce cocked her head. "What's that about?"

Cam playfully glared at Sandy. "Go ahead and tell her the rest of the story, jabber jaws."

"I commented that Cam's kitchen could use a woman's touch the other day. Cam's not the greatest at eating on a routine basis." Sandy shrugged.

"I would be delighted to show you my talents in the kitchen, Ms. St. Angelo," Luce told Cam.

"Whenever you're ready, I'm willing," Cam tossed back.

"Tuesday night it is then," Luce said. "You do own pots and pans, right?"

"Yes, ma'am, I have dishes, too. Silverware and glasses," Cam informed her.

"Well, there ya go," Sandy snickered.

"Don't you have some fish to catch?"

"Yeah, I do. Have fun, you two," Sandy said, as she tucked Amite in her shirt and called to Willow.

"She won't be able to carry him like that for much longer," Luce remarked.

Cam shook her head. "Not as fast as he's going to grow. Are you ready for a tour?"

"I'll introduce you to my sisters after showing you my kitchen. If there is something I need, just let me know, and I'll get Karen to pick it up in town tomorrow." Cam started walking toward her home.

"As long as you've got the basics, I'm good. I'll bring whatever I plan to feed you so it can be a surprise."

Cam swung the door open to her home. "If we're out on the water when you arrive, just make yourself at home. Here's the kitchen, so you can look around to see if you need anything."

Luce surveyed the kitchen equipment and seemed pleased. Cam cringed when she opened the refrigerator, fearing it would be empty. She was shocked to find food filling several shelves. *Thank you, Wanda, or Karen, or whoever.*

"This will work," Luce replied and closed the door.

Cam gave her a quick tour of the house, and then they walked over to Wanda and Liz's. "This was the original home place where we grew up. Teresa, Karen, and I have built our homes on the property, so Wanda, Liz, and Sandy live here. Sandy sometimes stays over on the island, as do I."

"What's the island?" Luce asked.

"It's an island across the bayou that our family has owned a large portion of for years. That will be part of our tour. We have a small cabin that we use when we are doing a guided hunt or just need a fun getaway."

"What kind of hunts?" Luce asked as they walked.

"Mostly white-tailed deer and wild hogs. The hog population exploded years ago, and we hunt them regularly to cull the population. We have an annual pig pickin at the end of the year after a big hunt, and provide meat for families in the community who need extra protein. They graciously return the kindness with extra vegetables and fruits that they grow."

Luce smiled softly at Cam, obviously impressed by the family.

As they stepped into the house, Wanda and Liz were sipping coffee in the kitchen. "Good morning, ladies. Would you care for some coffee?" Liz asked.

Luce looked at Cam. "Do we have time?"

"We have all day. Two cups, please, ma'am."

Wanda held out her hand. "I'm Wanda, and this gorgeous woman is my wife, Liz. It's a pleasure to meet you finally."

"You too." She looked at Liz. "I think I've seen you at the hospital, haven't I?" Luce asked Liz.

"Yes, I'm a trauma nurse there. You do look familiar, but you're usually in a uniform."

"That would be me," Luce answered.

"Luce is coming out to cook dinner for me Tuesday," Cam announced. "So, don't be surprised if I'm not home, but someone is in my house."

"Well, I'm glad someone is going to put that kitchen to good use finally," Wanda teased. "You've got every gadget and widget known to man, but you rarely cook."

Cam smirked. "Don't have to when I've got family that cooks like y'all."

Liz handed them coffee. "She talks big, but she's a sweetheart and can cook when she chooses."

"It's easier just to roll in after a long day and make a sandwich or something simple," Cam said in her defense.

"Yeah, but you've lost too much weight. We need you strong for gator season," Wanda said.

"I'm still as strong as ever," Cam replied.

"Maybe so, but I'd be happy to see ten pounds on ya," Liz said.

"Y'all gonna tag team me now?" Cam groaned.

"Nope. I'll say no more," Wanda grinned. "Until tomorrow, at least. I know you'll eat well tonight."

†

Sandy drove the boat to one of her favorite spots and cast her line. She watched a heron as his head darted under the water and returned with a frog in its beak. "Well, that's one Karen's boys won't catch." Sandy knew how much the boys enjoyed going out frog gigging at night. Heck, any excuse to be out on the water was fine with her. The water lapped gently against the boat as she waited for a bite. Willow dozed on a front bench, and Amite had curled up in the seat beside her. Sandy slowly reeled in her line as she watched an eagle soar in the distance. The island had been home to several nesting pairs for years, and she never tired of watching them glide so elegantly through the air.

She was deep in thought when the first tug at her line caught her attention. She set the hook and started fighting the fish. Even the smallest of catfish put up a good fight, making them one of the most fun to fish for, in Sandy's opinion. She began fighting the fish and grabbed the net to scoop her catch into the boat. Sandy was reeling in her third fish when she heard the roar of the airboat motor as Cam drove toward the Island. She tossed up her hand, and Cam waved back, a big smile on her face. Sandy cast her line.

"Two more, and we can head home," she told the animals.

†

When Sandy pulled up at the dock, Buster walked out to meet her. "Jeff and I will clean those for you if you'd like."

"That would be awesome, Buster. I can work on setting up the cookers."

"Nope, we got those ready, too," Buster replied. "We are so ready to cook for y'all."

"Okay, I'll go check with the ladies to see if they need my help," Sandy said as she handed the buckets of fish to him.

"We've got the beer ice cold, too, if you want one."

Sandy stepped off the boat. "No wonder my sisters married you two."

"Ha! We're the lucky ones," Buster replied. "Will you have some watermelon ready next week?"

"Yes, and something brand new for you to try out, too."

"A new blend?"

"Yes, several. Honeydew, apple pie, and pineapple-strawberry mix. I'll draw you up a quart of each to try. They'll be ready before y'all head back out."

"Those sound delicious," Buster grinned. "I can't wait."

"I'll see you in a bit. Thanks for skinning the cats."

"No problem. We'll go ahead and filet and bring in for soaking."

"Perfect." Sandy walked by the covered pavilion and grabbed a cold Abita from the ice cooler before walking into the house.

She could hear laughter coming from the kitchen as she entered. Liz and Wanda were covered in flour when she walked in. "What on earth? Is this a new type of foreplay?"

Liz spun around to look at Sandy and laughed. "No, but that's not a bad idea. We were just making the cakes for tonight, and our mixing got a bit out of hand."

"So, I see." Sandy took a seat at the counter and took a drink of beer. "Is there anything I can help with?"

"Nope, we've pretty much got everything under control except for the mixer." Wanda chuckled.

Sandy had tucked Amite into her shirt, and he poked his head out when he heard all the laughter. She pulled him out of her shirt and placed him on the floor. He ran around the counter to see what was going on and slipped in the flour coating the tile. Amite stood up, covered in the white flour, and sneezed.

"Oh, my goodness," Liz said as she scooped him up and tried to wipe the flour from his coat. Her attempt spread the flour over more of the kitten.

"Well, I guess I know what my next job is. I've got a kitten that now needs a bath." Sandy reached for him. "Should I wait until you two get done playing house?"

"Go ahead and bathe him in the bathroom sink. I'll clean up here so we don't have to wash, rinse, and repeat," Liz said, breaking out in laughter.

Sandy cocked an eyebrow. "Y'all haven't been eating any funny brownies or dipping into the shine, have you?"

"Nope, Squirt, just having a great time with the woman I love," Wanda replied.

"Nothing wrong with that." Sandy drained her beer. "I guess it's time we get acquainted with some water, little boy."

"Good luck," Liz said.

"Thanks, I'm probably going to need it." Sandy walked to the hallway bathroom and closed the door before sitting Amite on the floor. She grabbed some natural shampoo from the shower and ran some warm water in the sink. She picked Amite and kissed him on the nose. "This won't take long if you'll work with me."

Sandy was surprised by how well Amite did with his first bath. She lathered him and rinsed him without any loss of blood. Then she tucked him in a bath towel to dry him while the water drained.

"You did well, Amite." Sandy kissed his head and cuddled with him. "You smell good too." When he was dry, she picked him up and started back toward the kitchen.

"All clear in there?" she asked.

"Yes, we're good," Liz called back.

Sandy set him down on the floor, and Amite ran into the living room and pounced on Willow, who licked his head.

"Hey, now, I just got him clean and dry, don't get him all slobbery."

Amite curled up with Willow to watch the activity in the kitchen.

"Smells delicious in here."

"Did you eat anything today?" Wanda asked.

"I had a pack of crackers while I was out fishing."

"Lord, I swear Cam is such a bad influence on you," Wanda teased. "Ham or turkey sandwich?"

"Whatever is easier," Sandy replied.

Liz tossed her a bag of chips. "Tea or a soda?"

"Tea, please," she answered. "I can make my sandwich."

"I've got it. There's no room for a third person in this kitchen. I wonder how things are going with the lovebirds?" Wanda asked.

"I saw them headed to the island earlier. They were both smiling, so I reckon that's a good thing."

"Sounds like it," Liz said. "I don't know anyone who can resist the St. Angelo charm once it's turned on."

"You got that right, baby," Wanda said as she kissed Liz on her way to the refrigerator.

†

"I hope you don't mind me doing a bit of work this afternoon," Cam said as they walked toward a Gator. "I thought we could take a ride back into the Island and fill some deer feeders."

"That's perfectly fine. This place is beautiful," Luce replied.

"Grab a seat then." Cam loaded two bags of deer corn into the rear of the Gator. She climbed behind the wheel and drove slowly down the worn path. "If we're lucky, we might see some babies."

"Like those," Luce said, pointing toward a pair of fawns.

"Exactly like those. I could sit and watch the fawns play for hours. They are so cute when they are little."

"I know they are wild animals, but I don't think I could shoot one of them," Luce said.

"We don't overhunt, but it's important to cull the population of deer and wild hogs to keep the environment rich enough to support wildlife. I only take a few hunters after deer, but the hogs are a different story. They are very destructive and endanger the food sources of many other animals on the island."

"I could shoot a wild hog, I think," Luce answered.

"You'll get your chance later this year if you're interested. We usually have one to two hunts between the holidays to provide meat for families needing extra help. It's a win-win for all of us."

"So, the stories I've heard about the St. Angelo's being angels is true?" Luce asked, smiling.

"No angels, but our parents taught us to take care of others when we can, and providing meat is an easy way for us to do that. Sandy often fishes for several families as well. That kid loves to fish."

"I hate to break the news, but Sandy's not a kid anymore. She's a beautiful young woman."

"I know, but Squirt will always be my baby sister, no matter how old we are."

"I understand, but I couldn't resist a chance to tease you. Isn't hog hunting fairly dangerous?"

"You have to be careful and always hunt in pairs. They can be extremely aggressive animals." As Cam drove farther into the heart of the island, she pointed out several areas where the hogs had rooted up large regions of foliage. "They eat everything down to the roots, leaving nothing to grow back. We're going to reduce the numbers this year to enable us to replant some areas drastically affected by the hogs. No sense in planting if they come right behind us and devour what we've done."

"That makes good sense."

Cam pulled to a stop in front of two metal feeders and stepped out of the Gator. "I'll be right back."

Luce watched as Cam lifted a bag of corn and used a knife to cut it open. The sound of corn hitting the empty metal feeder made quite a racket. Cam returned for the second bag to fill the remaining bin.

"That's done. Would you like to stop by the cabin and have a sandwich? All this fresh air has made me hungry."

"Sure, that sounds good," Luce replied.

"Then we can head home and see how things are coming along for supper." Cam stored the empty bags and started driving.

When they pulled the Gator back under the shelter, Luce pointed out the crow's nest built in a tree near the water. "What's that for?"

"It has a multitude of uses. We built it years ago as a pirate's escape for Sandy, and now Karen's boys love playing in it. We can use it to scope out gators and fishing boats on the bayou, and it has a beautifully romantic view of the sunset over the bayou."

"I bet you've been up there once or twice with a woman," Luce said.

"Possibly," Cam stated. "It's got a fantastic view. If I had the talent to paint, it would make the perfect studio." She unlocked the door and opened it for Luce.

"This is nice," Luce said, looking around the cabin.

"We house our hunt guests here when we go for white-tailed deer, and it's an excellent place to get away for a weekend. Sandy and I spend time out here during the season. I lived here for a bit while my house was under construction." Cam walked to the refrigerator and opened the door. "Let's see. Ham, turkey, or bologna?"

"Bologna is fine with me as long as you have mayonnaise and potato chips," Luce said.

"I wouldn't be a country girl if I didn't keep those on hand. Tea, soda, or beer?"

"Tea is good. Thanks."

Cam began bringing items from the kitchen to the table where Luce sat. "So, what do you think of our little slice of paradise?"

Luce twisted the top on the mayo and opened the loaf of bread to begin making sandwiches. "It is a paradise for sure. With the gardens you pointed out earlier, a family could live off what they grew, caught, or hunted for easily."

"That is the point of the family homestead. We shop in town for what we need, that we don't harvest from here and barter with others for goods they have in excess. We get eggs, poultry, fruits, and vegetables from some of our neighbors."

"I like to see how well the family works together. No one seems to complain about the hard work."

"We love what we do, so most of it doesn't seem like work to us. Hunting, fishing, and growing things have always been our way of life."

"You would love my memaw," Luce told Cam. "She loves to garden and always has excess for bartering. I think going to the markets keeps her young and socially active."

"It's a lifestyle that will keep you healthy as well. We have plenty of hard physical work and lots of time outside. I can't imagine any of us being able to thrive in an office environment where we had to be inside all the time."

Luce handed Cam a sandwich. She laughed when Cam opened the bread, placed several potato chips on the meat, and smashed them with the bread's top slice. "That makes it a perfect sandwich, doesn't it?"

Cam nodded. "I wouldn't have it any other way." She swallowed and looked at Luce. "I'd love to meet your memaw one day. Maybe you can invite her for the holidays."

"She would fall in love with this place and your family," Luce said.

Before Cam could filter her thoughts, the words slipped out of her mouth. "What about you?"

"It's too late for me. I think I've already fallen in love."

"That's wonderful to hear. We're no angels but are a hard-working, hard-playing bunch. I'd love to have you a part of this family."

"I'd like that too. I don't want to order a U-Haul yet, but I enjoy getting to know you."

"No need for a U-Haul anyhow," Cam teased. "We've got trucks and the muscle necessary to move you." She winked. "When we both agree the time is right."

They picked up from the meal, and when Cam turned back to Luce after placing items back in the fridge, Luce was smiling. "What?"

Luce stepped forward and took Cam in her arms, pressing their lips together in a soft kiss. Cam's lips parted, and Luce accepted the invitation to deepen the kiss. Moments later, when Luce broke the kiss and stepped backward, she was breathless.

"I've wanted to do that for weeks."

"I have, too, but I didn't want to rush anything," Cam admitted. She placed her hand on her chest. "My heart is for sure about to beat out of my chest."

"I don't work until the late shift tomorrow. Could we spend some time together after the boil tonight?

"I would love that. You are more than welcome to spend the night, especially once the beer starts flowing."

"Thank you. I packed a bag just in case I needed one." Luce grinned.

"Were you a Girl Scout?" Cam chuckled.

"No, but I do believe in being prepared."

"I like that. Are you ready to head back across the water? It'll soon be time to start cooking."

Cam locked the door behind them, and Luce held out her hand. Cam eagerly laced her fingers between Luce's as they walked back to the airboat. Cam stopped short of climbing into the boat and turned for another kiss.

"Now I think I can make it across the water."

"It would be my pleasure to help in any way I can," Luce replied.

†

Sandy watched as Cam and Luce pulled into the boat slip and parked the airboat. Her face broke into a grin when she watched Cam reach for Luce's hand to help her off the boat, and they didn't release hands as they walked toward the pavilion.

"How was the grand tour?" she asked Luce.

"This place is amazing," Luce said. "We saw fawns, gators, and lots of other wildlife. I can see why you all love it out here."

"She even wants to join us one day during gator season to see what it's like, and maybe even a hog hunt."

"That would be a lot of fun. I'm glad you enjoy our little slice of paradise. Did y'all see the eagles fishing?"

Cam frowned. "No, we missed them. They are always fun to watch."

"We've got several mated pairs that have lived in these parts for a long time," Sandy informed Luce.

"We'll have to keep a better eye for the eagles next time," Luce said.

Cam bumped shoulders with Sandy. "Maybe we should fish with Sandy. She always sees them. Do you like to fish?"

"Does a frog bump his butt when he hops?" Luce asked.

"Oh, my word, I haven't heard that in forever," Sandy declared.

"Are you about ready to start cooking?"

"Just waiting on you, boss. The boys have everything set up. The sides and desserts are all set. You want me to fire up the cookers and get the oil heating?"

"Sure, I can start the boudin while I'm mixing up the hushpuppies," Cam replied. She turned to Luce. "Do you mind helping me carry some stuff out?'

"Not at all. Lead the way," Luce replied.

Sandy watched them walk toward the house and saw how easily their hands came together as they walked. "Stepping it up a notch for sure."

†

Once the food started hitting the tables, the crowd gathered. With a beer in hand, Cam supervised Luce, who

146

wanted to take a shot at cooking the hushpuppies. "You're a natural," Cam praised as Luce scooped up the golden-brown treats as they began floating in the oil.

Sandy's filets turned out nicely, too, and it didn't take long for food to start disappearing off the platters. Buster and Jeff waited until a layer of paper covered the tables and then poured the first pot of boil into a large cooler. T and Karen filled platters full of corn, potatoes, sausage, and crawfish. Plates of peanut-covered slaw accompanied each platter, and the family enjoyed the fantastic feast.

Cam and Sandy shut down their cookers and joined the meal. Luce and Liz had decided to split the last of the boudin rolls. When Luce was down to the last bite, Cam guided Luce's hand to her mouth to devour the bite.

"This is all so tasty," Luce said. "I don't ever think I've ever had such a collection of tastes all at one time."

Sandy raised her bottle of beer. "Welcome to the St. Angelo family pastime. We love cooking and eating with friends. Wait until you see this place during a pig pickin. Half the town will stop by for a plate or two."

"I can't wait," Luce said. "I know you said you cull the herd and share the meat with families, but how do you process all that meat at once?"

Sandy replied. "The crew at LB's processes them for the price of a hog apiece. They would do it for free, but Cam insists we bring them each a nice hog."

"Buster and Jeff use two or more of the biggest hogs and cook them for up to fourteen hours in our special setup.

When the meat is finished cooking, it is so tender and flavorful, and there's nothing else like it." Cam took a bite of corn.

"What kind of wood do they use?" Luce asked.

"Oak and apple wood. One of our neighbors has an old orchard that doesn't produce much anymore, and when he plants new trees, he cuts down the old ones and cuts it to length for us to use in the cooker." Sandy grinned. "Cam had an idea a few years ago to buy the man a chainsaw. He now cuts the lengths we used to have to chop as kids."

Luce looked at Cam. "That was smart."

"One of the best investments I ever made," Cam replied.

Liz returned to the table with a fresh round of beer. "Y'all already dreaming of the pig pickin? I swear half of the hospital staff show up out here."

"If the volunteer firemen can't make it, we take or send plates for them. Many families in town are fed by us that weekend," Wanda chimed in. "It's a great way to end the old year and start the new."

†

When the boil started to wrap up around eleven, Cam and Luce bid the sisters goodnight and walked to her home. Sandy, Wanda, and Liz were still seated around the campfire.

Sandy looked at Wanda. "I do believe big sister is about to ramp things up a notch."

"It's about damn time," Wanda growled. "I've never known Cam to be so patient."

"I think Cam wants to make sure Luce is the right one. You were worth the wait, my love," Liz said as she leaned over to kiss Wanda.

Wanda kissed her wife. "That was a lovely thing to say. Are you about ready to hit the sack?"

"With you? I'm always ready," Liz said with a wink to Sandy. "You coming in, Squirt?"

"After I finish this beer and dowse the fire. I promise to be quiet."

"We may not be." Wanda laughed. "See you in the morning for breakfast."

"Goodnight." Sandy took another sip of the beer. Watching her sisters depart with the women they loved did leave an ache in her heart. She scooped up Amite and placed him in her lap. "Maybe one day soon, you'll have a second mama." Amite curled in her lap and started purring.

Sandy looked up in time to see a shooting star as it raced across the sky. "I know what I wish for tonight."

†

Luce grabbed a small bag from her car and followed Cam inside into her bedroom. Cam placed the duffle on the hope chest at the end of the bed. She took Luce in her arms and kissed her deeply. "Thank you for joining us today."

"I had a wonderful time, and I hope it's not over yet," Luce replied.

"Shower with me? I need to get some of this smoke off me."

"I hoped you'd ask. I'd love to."

Cam kicked off her boots and was starting to unbuckle her jeans when Luce stepped forward. "Wait, I want to do that." Cam nodded.

Luce began to undress Cam, allowing her eyes to devour every inch of skin as her hands exposed it. Cam's body was beautifully proportioned and powerfully built. Her hands lowered Cam's jeans, revealing long, muscular legs. Luce tossed the jeans toward a hamper and carefully looped her fingers beneath the waistband of Cam's underwear, sliding them down the smooth legs. Cam stepped out of them as Luce stood. Luce's fingers floated up Cam's sides, feeling the heated skin as she lifted the T-shirt over Cam's head. Luce kissed the bare skin between Cam's neck and shoulder, eliciting a soft moan from Cam.

Cam's body was vibrating with excitement as Luce undressed her. She could see the fire of desire burning in Luce's eyes as they explored her body. When Luce removed Cam's sports bra and kicked off her shoes, that was Cam's cue to undress Luce. She had waited weeks for this moment, and now that it had arrived, Cam was nervous. The first time with Tab had been one of the best nights of her life, and Cam wanted tonight to feel just as memorable. Her fingers trembled with excitement as she reached down to unfasten Luce's belt and lowered her pants to allow her to step out of them. Luce was only an inch shorter than Cam, so pulling her shirt and sports bra off with one movement was easy. Cam allowed her eyes to roam across Luce before pulling their bodies together. Skin to skin, they molded together perfectly into a deep kiss. Cam enjoyed making love in the shower, but that would have to wait. She took Luce's hand and led her into the bathroom. Once under the warm water flow, Cam teased Luce's body with the soapy washcloth's gentle strokes. She was unsure who elicited the moans echoing in the shower. Cam rinsed Luce's body and couldn't resist a flick of her tongue across Luce's hardened nipple.

Luce grinned at Cam. "That was cruel. Turn around and spread 'em, against the wall."

"Yes, Deputy," Cam replied and turned away from Luce, placing her hands on the wall and spreading her feet.

Luce lathered the cloth and started at the base of Cam's neck, slowly swirling down her back. Cam's buttocks, beautifully round, led to the powerful legs Luce had admired earlier. She washed the backside and reached around to begin the front. Luce caressed Cam's breast with the soft lather, and could feel her nipples tensing under her touch. As the cloth moved south, Luce stepped closer, the soapy cloth sliding inside Cam's thighs brushing against Cam's center. Her thumb brushed across Cam's opening, and Luce heard her catch her breath. Luce lifted her hands to straighten Cam's stance as Luce pressed Cam's body into the front of hers. She nipped at Cam's shoulder and then moved her mouth to Cam's ear.

"I can't wait any longer. I need to be naked in your bed right now."

Cam turned to face Luce and kissed her deeply as she maneuvered their bodies under the water flow. She turned off the water and grabbed towels.

Cam took Luce into her bedroom, gently pressing her onto the bed with her body on top. Their bodies moved together in a primal rhythm as their tongues danced in a fevered kiss. They both released the build-up of excitement, and Cam moved to lay beside Luce to begin making slow passionate love to Luce. The urgency to release gone, Cam enjoyed raising Luce's desire with gentle teasing and caresses as she explored every curve and contour of Luce's body.

They made love for hours before Cam curled around Luce's body for much-needed rest. Cam was confident they would both sleep with smiles on their faces.

†

Sandy returned to the dock from resetting the crawfish traps when she saw Cam walking Luce to her car. When Luce turned for a goodbye kiss, Sandy was sure both of them were oblivious to anything or anyone around them. They certainly didn't see the sheriff's cruiser rolling by the drive or the flash of the mirrored glasses Bugsy always wore.

"Well shit, I guess that game is on."

Ever since Bugsy had arrived in town, she had stalked Cam, who pushed her attention aside. With Luce in the picture, Sandy knew Bugsy would make life uncomfortable for Cam and Luce. "Maybe time for you to kick her ass, once and for all." Sandy grinned. She knew Cam wouldn't resort to violence, but there was more than one way to skin a cat. Sandy watched the cruiser speed away and then began loading her fishing gear.

Today would be the last restful day of fishing before the gator season started, and she wanted to haul in a massive bounty for Hank at LB's to hold them through at least the first week or two of the seasons. Sandy hoped Cam would join her, but a quick look toward Luce's car still found Cam leaning in, talking to Luce.

"This could be an hour," Sandy groaned and stomped off toward the house.

"I thought you left already," Wanda said.

Sandy shrugged. "I was hoping Cam would join me for a day of fishing, but she's still saying goodbye to Luce."

"Shoot her a text. If you're willing to wait a few more minutes, I bet she'll go. Fix a thermos of coffee to take with you while you wait."

Sandy pulled out her phone and shot Cam a text.

Gimme five minutes, Cam sent back.

"Yes!" Sandy pumped her fist in the air. "Would you mind if I take some of these leftover biscuits and ham?"

"Knock yourself out," Wanda said. "I'll bag them up while you make coffee."

CHAPTER EIGHT

Sandy waited as patiently as she could at the dock for Cam.

"Okay, so it was a bit past five minutes," Cam said as she climbed aboard the boat.

"That's all right. I was enjoying one of Wanda's country ham biscuits," Sandy replied, popping the last bite in her mouth. She paused to take a sip of coffee.

"Those look good. Did you bring extras?"

"Two more in the bag for you. Your coffee's already in your mug. I was hoping you'd help me bring in a bunch of catfish today."

Cam dug into the bag and pulled out a foil-wrapped biscuit, and took a bite. "Damn, this tastes great. Thanks for the coffee, too." Cam took a sip. "I wouldn't miss a chance to fish with you. Today will probably be our last day of relaxing. We've still got several batches of shine to cook and deliver while getting our gear ready for gator season to start."

"I think everyone was pleased with how well the new flavors turned out," Sandy replied. "I was surprised at how well the pineapple and strawberry tasted, especially the batch we made with the pineapple juice instead of fresh fruit."

Cam swallowed. "Using the juice will speed things up a bit while holding down the costs. Have you given the names some thought?"

"I was thinking Bayou Dew for the honeydew melon batch."

"Not bad. What about the apple pie?"

"That one was much harder. I haven't settled on one yet. I was thinking Island Delight for the pineapple and strawberry." Sandy pulled away from the dock as Cam started on the second biscuit.

"How about American Pie?"

"Nothing more American than baseball, hotdogs, and apple pie." Sandy chuckled.

"So, they say." Cam grinned.

"Sounds good to me. I'll text Karen and get her to print out a bunch of labels. She and T can place them on the jars, jugs, and buckets while we cook." Cam pulled out her phone and a smile grew on her face.

"Luce already missing you?" Sandy teased.

"No, another Texas order. They loved the fresh flavors and want ten gallons of everything we can make this week."

"Even at the increased prices?" Sandy asked.

"Yep, they understand the cost of the fruit and melons is high this year."

"We cooking tonight then?"

"I think we need to get a jump on this order if we plan to deliver before gator season starts. We've got a bunch of mash ready for cooking, too."

Sandy pulled into one of her favorite spots. "Better get to fishing then."

"Ten dollars for the biggest fish?" Cam challenged Sandy.

"Get your ten dollars ready for my pocket then." Sandy cast her line across the water.

†

After delivering the catfish to LB's, Sandy and Cam started for home. Wanda had cooked a hearty meal and met them at the dock when she heard them approaching.

"I assume you two will be cooking tonight, so I made supper. Do you want to eat here or take it to the island with you?"

Cam pulled out a ten and handed it to Sandy. "I think we have time to eat here."

"Thanks, Cam," Sandy said and tucked the bill in her pocket.

Wanda cocked her head. "Squirt won again?"

"She always does." Cam slung an arm over Sandy's shoulders. "Let's go eat."

When they stepped inside the house, Sandy breathed deeply. "Fried chicken, rice, and gravy?"

"With some leftover coleslaw and cake from last night," Wanda answered.

"I may have to nap while you cook after eating all this." Cam took a seat beside Wanda.

"It wouldn't hurt either of you to get some extra sleep when possible this week. Starting Sunday, it will be nonstop until we fill all our tags."

"There will be plenty of time to sleep after gator season." Sandy grinned at Cam. She had heard her sister utter those words many times.

Little did Sandy or anyone know how the next month would change their lives forever.

"Dig in," Liz said and took a piece of chicken from the plate and passed it to Sandy.

Sandy filled her plate. Something was missing, and when she walked to the pantry and pulled out a jar of dry roasted peanuts, Wanda nodded.

"I knew I was missing something." Wanda waited until Sandy poured the peanuts over her slaw and then passed the jar around the table. "I can't eat slaw without them anymore."

†

Cam and Sandy cooked every night that week and made a late-night run to deliver a massive order to their Texas connection. Cam reminded him that gator season was starting and production would slow to a halt, but they would resume cooking as soon as possible.

Two weeks into the season, the Gator Girlz were rolling along, meeting or exceeding their daily tag quotas at every turn. With Karen and T's help, they had cooked a few batches of shine. Sandy had convinced Cam to allow her and Wanda to make a trip to meet a Baton Rouge customer while Cam filled some local orders and then return home for some sleep.

Cam saw Wanda and Sandy off safely with their order and tucked two gallons of the Red Bliss into a cooler in the back floorboard of the Jeep. Then she drove to town and made the first delivery with no problems. Cam began the trip to the far side of town to make her final delivery and was five minutes from her destination when blue lights filled the air.

"Shit. Please be Luce," she prayed. Her heart sank when she saw the much shorter figure of Bugsy step from the cruiser and walk her way.

The events that unfolded that night nearly ended the blossoming relationship between Luce and Cam when Bugsy found the shine she was transporting and arrested her for possession and transporting illegal alcohol. Cam had failed to inform Luce of the moonshine business the family ran from the island in fear that the knowledge would end the relationship, but learning it from Bugsy made everything chaotic. Luce had listened to Cam's explanation but left town to clear her head, feeling betrayed and humiliated by Cam's behavior. Thankfully, Luce's memaw was patient and helped Luce see the issue from a different angle, and together they came up with a solution to propose to Cam. Memaw's suggestion on creating a legitimate business for the moonshine was brilliant, and Luce would not feel she was betraying her oath to uphold the law if the company was legal and licensed.

When Luce finally returned and proposed the business's legalization, Cam was relieved that Luce had returned and was at least willing to talk with her. Her heart had shattered from the look in Luce's eyes when she had last seen her and feared their relationship had ended. Luce had not forgiven Cam for the mistrust, but her heart was invested enough in Cam to try to work things out between them.

Cam was a hot mess when Luce had walked out, and Sandy and her sisters had worked hard to support her during the trauma. Cam had slept very little during the previous week, and the exhaustion was evident in her appearance and energy level. Sandy tried to keep her focused on the work, but Cam was irritable and distracted. After talking, the sisters decided a day off from hunting was needed for rest. Cam was resistant to the idea but overruled by her sisters. Wanda cooked hot meals for her, and Cam was encouraged to get as much sleep as possible.

Sandy was so concerned that she decided to text Luce to plea for Luce to come to dinner and spend the night. When they arrived at LB's to drop a load of gators, Sandy informed Cam she needed to use the restroom and would be back in a few minutes. She pulled out her phone and went to work.

Hey, Luce, this is Sandy.

Hey, Squirt. What's up?

I'm worried about Cam. Since this issue with the moonshine has come up between you, she hasn't slept well. I worry about her health and Cam's inability to focus on our dangerous work when she's so physically exhausted. We don't need Cam or anyone else getting hurt. I may be out of place here, but I need to ask if you can help.

What can I do?

Come to dinner tonight and spend some time talking with Cam, so she knows she has a future with you if you feel you have one, or cut her loose so she can move on. Cam can't function like this, and we need her leadership.

Sandy waited for several minutes for Luce to respond. She held her breath when she finally saw Luce was writing an answer.

I'm not completely over this ordeal, but I do love Cam and want to make a go of a life with her. I didn't realize how physically affected she was by all this drama.

She's a hot mess right now.

I'll come for dinner tonight and talk with her. Maybe she will relax enough to sleep.

Thank you, Luce. See you at seven?

That's perfect.

Sandy breathed a sigh of relief and shot a text to Wanda. *We're on for dinner tonight at seven.*

Good deal. Liz is off tonight, so I'll get her to start dinner for us. I know we can all use a break tomorrow.

Sandy was smiling when she returned to the boat to find Cam talking with Hank. "Hey, Hank."

"Hi there, Squirt, did everything come out all right in there," he teased.

"You may want to block off that restroom for a bit," Sandy shot back at him. She stepped onto the boat and handed Cam a cold Sun Drop soda. "Man, these are exceptionally cold today."

"I decided to put a six-pack in the freezer in case you wanted some today. The drinks have been thawing since I opened at five."

"Thanks, Hank. We needed something cold. It's been a hot day and no breeze to speak of to loosen the blanket of humidity," Sandy replied.

Hank ran a hand across his brow. "I hear ya. At least I can sneak into the office for a few minutes of cold air. It must be brutal under the direct sun."

"It's not getting any cooler. Let's go run the rest of our lines for the day. I'm ready for a cold beer and bed," Cam admitted.

Sandy climbed into the driver's seat. "Let's roll. See ya later, Hank."

"Y'all be safe out there," Hank said and waved goodbye.

After hauling in a dozen more gators, Cam and Sandy started for home. "I guess I need to tell you now that Luce is joining us for dinner at seven."

"What?" Cam asked, confused.

"I invited her to dinner with us. Liz is cooking, and we need a relaxing evening."

"Yes, that we do. Thanks for thinking of that. My mind has been all over the place the last week or so."

Sandy pulled the airboat into the slip and tossed Cam the rope to tie them off. "So, get cleaned up and join me for a cold beer under the pavilion until she arrives."

Cam looked at her watch. "It's almost six already."

"It won't take either of us long to clean up. Just don't preen in front of the mirror too long," Sandy teased.

"Okay, smartass. I'll see you in a bit," Cam said as they parted ways, and she walked into her house.

Wanda was already home and cleaned up when Sandy entered. "Did you break the news to Cam about Luce coming out and taking tomorrow off?"

"Luce, yes, but I'm going to hit her with the day off after we've eaten. She'll be less apt to argue in front of Luce."

Liz looked up from the stove. "You are so wicked. But I love it."

"Great idea. Get cleaned up. I've got a few cold ones in the freezer chilling for y'all."

"Thanks, Wanda, and thanks for cooking dinner on short notice, Liz."

"Anything to help," Liz answered and stirred the pot of food she was preparing.

161

†

Cam undressed and looked at her image in the mirror. "Damn girl, you look tired." The circles under her eyes had grown darker. "I need a good night's sleep." Cam relaxed in the hot shower, then dressed in shorts and a Gator Girlz T-shirt before joining Sandy under the pavilion.

"You certainly smell better," Sandy teased when she handed Cam a bottle of beer.

"That shirt looked tie-dyed that I took off with all the salt stains," Cam replied. "It sure was a hot one today, and tomorrow isn't looking any cooler."

"Tis the season." Sandy chuckled and tapped the neck of her bottle with Cam's.

"We are up to two hundred eighty after today's haul," Cam replied. "If we tag out early, what do you think of picking up a few extra tags? Hank mentioned a few hunters today struggling to fill their tags."

"It would be a win-win. We get the extra income, and the hunter gets to keep the tag allotment for next year."

"That's what I was thinking. Maybe we can use the extra income for a vacation fund." Cam watched Sandy's face. "Maybe go on a cruise or something?"

"That would be a lot of fun. Let's start researching some ideas." Sandy turned her head at the sound of tires crunching on the gravel driveway. She saw Luce pull in next to the Jeep.

Cam stood and handed Sandy the empty bottle. "We'll be inside in a few. Thanks for the beer."

"Don't be long. I'm hungry," Sandy warned.

"We won't be."

Sandy walked into the house as Cam went to meet Luce.

†

"Hey, I'm so glad you could join us tonight." She wrapped Luce in a hug and was relieved when Luce kissed her.

"I'm glad for the opportunity to see y'all. I miss you," Luce replied.

"I hope you know you can come out anytime," Cam said as she reached for Luce's hand. "We have to go. Sandy's hungry as a bear tonight."

"I'm right behind her. I forgot about lunch today." Luce replied.

"How do you forget about lunch?"

"The same way you do. You get so busy that by the time you know it, lunchtime is way past."

"Guilty as charged, officer," Cam said as she pulled the door open.

Liz was pouring tea as Wanda and Sandy were placing dishes of food on the table.

"Damn, it smells good in here," Cam said as they entered.

"My goodness, what a spread," Luce said. "Fried pork chops, rice, and gravy. Are those collard greens and cornbread, too? I have died and gone to heaven."

"Corn casserole will be up in a minute," Liz said. "Go ahead and get started, and I'll be right over."

†

Sandy was the last to push her plate away. "That was beyond delicious, Liz. Thanks for cooking."

"You're more than welcome. Are we ready for some coffee and cake?" Liz asked as she walked to the kitchen to pull down coffee mugs.

"Why do I always forget about dessert?" Sandy grumbled. "I'm sure I can make a spot. Do you need some help?"

"Nope, sit tight. I've got this. Wanda, will you slice some cake?"

"Sure thing, Babe," Wanda said and shot a look at Sandy.

"Cam, the sisters and I have talked, and we believe we all need a rest day tomorrow," Sandy blurted out.

Cam opened her mouth to speak, but Sandy continued.

"We are all exhausted, and we are ahead of schedule filling tags. One day off won't keep us from reaching that goal."

"I don't have a problem with that, but don't expect me to laze around all day in bed," Cam informed them.

"I bet I could convince you to stay in bed a little longer than usual," Luce said with a wiggle of her eyebrows.

Cam nearly choked on the drink of tea she had taken. She looked at Luce and nodded. "If there is anyone in the room that could, it would be you."

"Well, you did say I could visit anytime, so I'm off the next two days. Maybe we could both relax tomorrow, and the following day, I can go gator hunting with y'all?"

"Oh, hell yeah," Sandy said and gave Luce a high five.

"I reckon I'm a bit outnumbered here, so yes, a day off sounds great."

"All right," Wanda said as she began passing slices of cake. "I'll make that lasagna I promised you for dinner tomorrow night."

"That's too good to pass up. You know, I was talking with Hank today, and he mentioned a few hunters were having difficulty filling their tags, and he wanted to see if we wanted to pick some up? Sandy and I discussed it earlier and thought it might be fun to use the extra revenue for a vacation fund. What do you think?"

Wanda took her seat and looked at Liz. "We've wanted to go on a cruise for years. Maybe one of the women-only ones. I think we could fill a few more tags after we meet our quota, so count me in. I'm sure T would agree to some extra income."

"Well, that's settled. I'll let Hank know we're interested when we get back to work." Cam speared a bite of cake and placed it in her mouth. "I'm feeling so much better already."

"You need to start coming home with Sandy and Wanda for a hot meal," Liz told her.

"I could start coming out to cook for you on days I work the early shift, too," Luce offered.

"That would be great. If you and Liz could do the fixings, I could grill us up a nice steak this weekend."

Sandy's eyes grew wide. "Hey, why don't we see if we can get our hands on some Royal Red shrimp and make it a surf-and-turf night?"

"That does sound delicious," Cam said. "Lordy, I can't be hungry after that meal, but I swear my stomach just growled."

"It remembers the taste of those shrimp." Sandy laughed.

"Those were fantastic. Some of the best I've ever tasted," Cam agreed.

"I'll give Hank a call tomorrow to see if he can get us some," Sandy said.

"Salad, corn, and maybe some broiled asparagus?" Luce suggested.

"I'll do a big salad and maybe some strawberry shortcake for dessert," Liz offered.

"I love it when a plan comes together." Sandy took a sip of coffee. "I've got my belly full, and I'm going to sleep so well tonight. Amite and Willow can snuggle in beside me, and poof, I'll be gone."

"I hear ya. Let me help you pick up here, and we'll be gone," Cam said.

"Nonsense, you two go. I've got this," Liz said.

Cam stood and hugged Liz. "Thank you for a great meal. It really hit the spot."

"Good. I have to work tomorrow, but I'll make biscuits in the morning before I go, and y'all can make breakfast to go with them." Liz started stacking the cake plates.

"We'll see you tomorrow then," Cam said and reached for Luce, and they walked out together.

"Hang on a sec," Luce said when they reached her car. She walked over and pulled out her overnight bag.

"You know, you can start leaving some clothes and stuff here if you'd like," Cam said.

"I'd like that," Luce replied.

When they arrived at Cam's, Cam excused herself to use the restroom while Luce changed into sleep clothes. Cam brushed her teeth and slipped into a large sleep shirt. "The bathroom's all yours she said."

"I'll be right back," Luce smiled and softly kissed Cam as she sat on the bed. "Get comfy."

Luce was only in the bathroom for a few minutes, but Cam was already asleep when she returned. The stress and exhaustion had left her face as she relaxed, and her lips curled into a smile. Luce turned off the lamp and climbed in beside Cam, snuggling close to the woman with whom she had fallen so deeply in love.

†

Cam's eyes opened, and she turned to find the bed empty. It was almost eleven, and she couldn't believe she had slept so late. The exhaustion was more severe than she realized. She remembered waking when she rolled over to find Luce lying close beside her. Cam had kissed Luce's forehead and drifted back to sleep.

She could hear soft sounds coming from the kitchen and walked in to find Luce at her stove. She looked up when she heard Cam enter.

"Sandy brought biscuits and country ham by earlier. I thought I'd whip us up some scrambled eggs to go with them."

"Sounds great. What can I do?"

"Pour a cup of coffee and some apple juice for us, then join me at the table," Luce answered.

Cam glanced out the window at the bright sunny day. "It looks like another scorcher out there."

"Yes, it's already in the nineties and humid to boot." Luce divided the eggs onto two plates and carried them to the table. She sat next to Cam. "Is there anything else you need?"

"Yes." Cam leaned forward for a kiss. "Now, I'm all set."

"Good. Let's eat." Luce took a bite and watched Cam take a long drink of juice. "You know, in this heat, you probably get dehydrated, which can add to your fatigue. What do you carry on the boats to drink?"

"Coffee, water, and sometimes sodas," Cam answered.

"It wouldn't hurt to add some Gatorade and juices in there, too," Luce replied. "Especially when it's this danged hot."

"If you want to take a drive into town, I'll buy a few cases," Cam said.

Luce nodded. "After that, I want you to take me to the island and show me this moonshine setup. Your license application should be coming through soon, by the way."

"We can do that. I probably need to check the feeders, too, if that's okay."

"No problem. I love riding around with you."

"Thanks for all you've done to make an honest businesswoman out of me," Cam told Luce.

"You'll have to thank my memaw. She was the one that helped me get to that point. Her husband was a bootlegger back in the day when they first met. She understands the importance of the revenue to this way of life."

"I'd like to meet her sometime. Does she travel?"

"Not often, but maybe after gator season is over, we can go spend a weekend with her."

"I'd like that." Cam answered.

"She'd love it here, so maybe we can convince her to come down for a few days, too."

"Sounds great. These eggs are delicious. What did you put in them?"

"Butter, a bit of milk, and parmesan cheese," Luce replied.

"Wonderful," Cam said and took another bite.

†

Cam and Luce walked into the main house. "We're going to ride to town for some Gatorade. Is there anything you need from the store?"

Sandy sat at the table eating a grilled cheese. "Will you pick up treats for Willow and Amite?"

"I could use a few loaves of fresh garlic bread," Wanda said.

"On it," Cam said. "Call if you think of anything else. We're going to ride over to the island and fill up the feeders, too, when we get back. Are we doing okay for deer corn?"

"It wouldn't hurt to pick up a few bags," Sandy answered.

"We'll see you in a while then. Thanks for the biscuits."

"You're welcome. Drive safe," Wanda called to them.

Cam stepped up into her truck and waited for Luce to buckle in. They were halfway into town when they passed a sheriff's cruiser with Bugsy behind the wheel. Bugsy threw her hand up, and Cam ignored her.

"What's the history between the two of you?" Luce asked.

"We were sports rivals in high school and ended up on the same team in college. Bugsy has had a crush on me since we were teens, and no matter how much I ignored her, I couldn't convince her I wasn't interested. It finally led to a physical altercation our freshman year in college, and Bugsy could have lost her scholarship and her spot on the team. It took a great deal to convince Coach not to boot her."

"She should have been grateful of that."

"You would think so. After Bugsy graduated, she took a job here, and you know the rest."

"So, she's been stalking you for years?"

"Pretty much in a harmless way, but I'm seriously considering giving her a beat down if I catch her off duty any time soon."

"Don't lower yourself to her standards. Scott pretty much reamed her out after she arrested you and put her on a short leash. He was very close to firing her right off the bat."

"Bugsy is just an irritant. Once we're legal, there's nothing she can do but ticket me for speeding." Cam smirked at Luce. "I admit I can have a heavy foot."

"I remember pulling you over for a warning."

"Sandy still says that's how you found out my name."

"Well, she was right, but don't tell her that. I had seen you around but didn't want to ask anyone who you were. So, I figured out a way to find out for myself."

"Clever girl. Sandy said I should have just offered you my number then."

"It would have been a bit easier, but we finally met," Luce said and reached for Cam's hand.

†

When they returned from the store, Sandy helped them unload. "I'll take a case of these to put in the cabin," Cam said.

"I'll carry the corn and drinks out. Do you want to take the airboat?"

"I could use some practice unless you want to drive us around." Cam knew that Sandy was just as restless as she was and needed a job to do. "You can stock drinks in the cabin while we drive out to fill the feeders."

Sandy looked at Luce. "Do you mind a third wheel?"

"You will never be a third wheel around us," Luce corrected her, and Sandy's face beamed.

"We'll store these drinks in my pantry and fridge and meet you at the boat." Cam smiled at her little sister. "Love you, Squirt."

"Love you more," Sandy replied and started carrying the bags of feed to the boat.

"You know you just made her day, right?" Cam told Luce.

"It's the truth. Sandy nor any other members of your family will ever be a third wheel in my eyes. I love you all."

"We love you, too," Cam said. She kissed Luce and picked up two cases. "Can you get the last one?"

"No problem." Luce chuckled and followed Cam into the house.

They stored the drinks and met Sandy at the boat after delivering the bread to Wanda. "We'll be back later," Cam said as they headed for the back door. "We're taking Squirt with us."

"Good, she's been pacing the floor all day waiting for something to do." Wanda laughed. "She is so much like you."

"Yes, she is," Cam agreed. "See ya."

"She does seem to be a miniature version of you," Luce said.

"Even worse than me. Sandy can't stand to be inside if there is something she can do outside. She could have had a full ride to college, but she didn't want to leave here. This bayou is where her heart is."

"There's nothing wrong with that," Luce replied.

Sandy cranked the engine and had them on the dock at the island in no time. "Let me grab the Gator, and we can load up, and I'll stock the cabin while you're gone."

Sandy jogged around the shine shack and returned, driving a gator. Cam handed her two of the bags of deer corn that she placed in the back. "Do you want your pistol?"

"May not hurt. The hogs can be aggressive this time of year," Cam replied.

Sandy unlocked the console on the boat and handed Cam her firearm. Cam clipped it on her belt and climbed into the four-wheeler. Cam kept her eyes open as she drove, for deer as well as wild hogs. They reached the feeder and emptied the corn and were on their way back when a young boar blocked the path ahead of them. Cam took her pistol out and hollered at the hog.

"Go on, get outta here," she said and revved the engine, but the hog refused to clear the trail. Cam inched forward, and when the boar started charging, she took a shot, striking him between the eyes. The boar stumbled but did not fall, so Cam shot again. This time the animal fell to the ground.

"Damn, are they usually this aggressive?" Luce asked.

"They can be, especially around breeding season. Being a young male makes him even more reckless." Cam pulled the gator to a stop beside him. "Will you help me load him?"

Cam and Luce struggled but managed to lift the heavy animal onto the back of the Gator.

"What are you going to do with him?" Luce asked.

"I'll get Sandy to run him over to LB's for processing. I'm sure he can find somebody that needs some meat. I'll give you the tour of the shine shack while she's gone."

"Sounds like a plan." Luce climbed inside the Gator.

Sandy was waiting for them on the porch when they pulled up. "I heard shooting." She looked into the back of the Gator. "I'm glad you took your pistol."

"Me too. The hog wouldn't move from blocking the trail and then charged toward them. Magnum one, hog zero, but it took two shots to bring him down." Cam stepped out of the vehicle. "Will you run him over to LB's to be processed? I'm sure he'll know someone who needs some fresh meat."

"Sure will. Then I'll come back to pick y'all up," Sandy said. "Drive over to the dock. He may be young, but he looks heavy."

"He's probably close to three hundred," Cam guessed.

They loaded him onto the front of the boat, and Sandy watched as the front dipped down. "Yep, he's a big boy."

"Better keep the pistol in case mama comes looking for him."

Cam laughed and watched Sandy pull away. She turned to find Luce smiling. "What?"

"You two are so good together. Was that hog not full grown?"

"No, a mature male in these parts can be around five hundred pounds. We try to cull them out before too many get that size. They are rooting demons, destroying everything in their path."

"Good grief. I bet those tusks could do some damage, too."

"They can gut a dog or human with one mean swipe. That's why you should never hunt them alone, and make sure you have enough gun power to bring one down. A rifle would have been more efficient, but I didn't think to bring one."

Cam rinsed the bed of the Gator and parked it under the covering. Then she pulled out a set of keys and opened the shine shack, and took Luce inside.

"Wow, this is bigger than I had imagined," Luce said. "Your family has been making it for a long time?"

"Probably over two hundred years," Cam replied. "Have a seat."

Luce sat beside Cam, and she explained the process of making the mash and cooking it to form moonshine. Luce listened intently to Cam and asked questions when she didn't understand the terminology Cam used.

"I only know of corn mash as moonshine, but it sounds like you have developed a variety of flavors. How do you come up with those ideas?"

Cam was impressed by the interest Luce was showing. "You can pretty much use anything that can ferment into moonshine. Fruits and corn have pretty much been our staples. Once we go legal, we may create brandy and other liquor types, but our business base will remain moonshine. That's what the St. Angelo family has marketed for years. Would you like to try a sample or two?"

Luce nodded her head. "I'd love to."

Cam pulled down a pint jar of American pie and opened it before handing it to Luce. "Take a small sip and hold it in your mouth for a few seconds before you swallow." Cam watched as Luce took a drink, and her eyes grew wide.

"Oh my gosh, that tastes just like taking a bite of apple pie. I can feel the kick of the alcohol when I swallow. What's next?"

"This one is going to be a best seller for women," Cam said as she spun the lid off the Island Delight. "Pineapple juice and strawberries."

Luce sipped. "I can see why ladies would like that. It's sweet without the bite of alcohol."

"There's still plenty of kick to it, so you have to sip it slowly," Cam said. "I like the next one." She handed Luce a jar of Bayou Dew. "It's made from honeydew melons."

Luce chuckled after tasting the sample. "I can see why you like it. What's your overall best seller?"

"The Red Bliss, a watermelon shine. That's the one I was delivering to Scott when Bugsy pulled me over. I tried to pass it off as watermelon wine, but even Bugsy knew better."

"I love watermelon."

Cam pulled down a jar of Bliss and handed it to Luce. "It's sweet, but it packs a punch."

"Woohoo, yes it does," Luce said. "I can ask this since you're going legit. How much do you get for this?"

"Everything except for the Island Delight is one hundred dollars a gallon. Because of the cost of the pineapple juice and strawberries, we get one-twenty-five a gallon."

"One run of the still produces how much?"

"Depending on the flavor, twelve to fifteen gallons. We will have to increase prices once we go legal to cover the taxes, but our regular customers won't hesitate to buy our alternative fuel." Cam chuckled.

"Wow," Luce said, nearly speechless. "I can see why so many people would take the risk."

"Back in the Depression and when times were hard, it was the only thing that kept some families fed. The risk of going to jail was less of a threat than a starving family."

"I never really thought of it in those terms," Luce admitted.

"I want to do some research and see if it would be feasible to add a small warehouse to the property and purchase a more considerable still. It can be a pain transporting mash and finished shine over the water sometimes."

"You can cook during the day, so you don't have to burn the candles at both ends to stay undetected. That does make sense."

"I've got a brain cell or two still functioning," Cam teased.

"I don't doubt that at all. You've created and maintained several family business ventures, and you do an excellent job of caring for your community. That's a special thing, in my opinion."

"Maybe once we go legit, I can teach you how to cook a batch."

"I think I'd like that. It seems like an exciting process. Maybe I could help with deliveries some days, too."

"Our shine goes as far west as Houston and at least to Jackson, Mississippi, to the east. Maybe farther. Once it leaves my hands, I can never tell." Cam stood when she heard the airboat approach. "Jeff and Buster typically take a gallon or two offshore when they go, so it's rare we have any stock unsold. It usually goes out as fast as we can deliver."

"I assume you and Sandy do most of the cooking and delivery?" Luce asked.

"Wanda and Liz help out too. Wanda, T, and Karen often cut the fruit and set up the mash. T and Karen print the labels and place them on the containers."

"So, it is a complete family business?"

"Yes, Jeff and Buster help by bringing sugar and other supplies when they come in from being offshore. Buying too much yeast, or sugar, or even fruit tends to raise some suspicion. The larger orders go into five-gallon buckets, and the customer can then break them down into smaller units to sell."

"Amazing," Luce said. She followed Cam, out of the shack, and they walked to the dock. "What about security on the island. I know it's remote but still accessible."

Cam pointed up to the crow's nest. "In addition to a fabulous make-out spot, the crow's nest has a view for miles. Add a pair of thermal detection binoculars, and we could see anyone coming for miles by water. By land, we have game cameras set up all over the island. Not only does it help to detect intruders, but the cameras also allow us to track the wildlife on the island for hunting."

"You are one smart cookie, St. Angelo," Luce said.

"Why, thank you, ma'am. I do try to work as efficiently as possible."

Sandy floated up to the dock. "Are you ladies set for a ride home?"

"Yes, Squirt, I think we are," Cam answered.

"Can we take one quick side trip?"

"Why not?" Cam nodded.

Sandy backed away from the dock and turned left, deeper into the bayou. A few seconds later, she killed the engine, and the boat floated quietly across the water.

"There." She pointed to the top of a cypress tree."

"Eagles," Luce whispered. They watched as a baby raised its head to eat. "A baby too."

"I saw one of them fishing earlier," Sandy replied softly. "The baby was a bonus."

"Good job, Squirt," Cam said. "Can you get us out of here quick so they can go back to feeding?"

"I can't be quiet, but I can be quick." Sandy turned the ignition and spun the boat quickly to leave the slough they had drifted into earlier.

When they approached the dock, Amite sat there patiently waiting. As Sandy pulled into the slip, she scooped him into her arms. "You sure are growing," she cooed and kissed the top of his head. "Were you waiting for mama to come home?"

Amite rubbed his head under Sandy's chin. "I think that's a yes," Cam replied.

Sandy looked over at Cam. "Are you two up for a fire in the pit tonight? I know we can't stay out late, but it's going to be a nice night."

"That sounds good. I see TJ and Billy coming down the drive from the school bus. I bet they'd help gather wood."

Sandy nodded. "You two go clean up and chill. I'll recruit the boys and give you a holler when dinner is ready."

"Sounds great. Thanks for the ride."

"My pleasure. I forgot to tell you that Hank will be splitting that hog up between a couple of families. He sends his thanks."

"That's good news. If anyone knows the needs of this community, it's Hank."

"Let's go talk with some boys," Sandy told Amite and placed him on her shoulder. "See ya."

Cam closed the door behind them. "Are you ready for a cold beer and an amazing sight?"

"I'm always ready for that."

"Let me go wash my hands, and I'll be right back."

Luce wandered through the living area, browsing photos while she waited on Cam. Several shots of the softball team and many pictures of Cam and a teammate were scattered through the room. She could tell the woman was very special to Cam and was studying one photo in particular when Cam walked back into the room.

"That's Tab and me during our last year together at school."

"Where is she now?"

"After finishing up law school at Duke, she moved back to Monroe," Cam answered. "She was my first love, but we only had a short time."

Luce could sense the emotion in Cam's voice. "Why are you not still together?"

Cam shrugged. "Different paths in life. After Mama died, Dad needed help raising my four sisters and running the family business. Tab's goal was to finish law school and return to Monroe to join her father or open a solo practice. My heart is here, and I didn't think we would survive a long-distance relationship."

"That must have been hard."

"It was at first. Parker, one of our teammates, got a graduate assistant position at Duke, so Tab at least had someone she knew. As fate would have it, they became more than friends and have been together a few years now. Parker coaches in Monroe." Cam sighed. "I returned home after the second year of studies, much wiser about business, and buckled down to ensure the family business, now the Gator Girlz, Inc., thrived."

"It sounds like you've sacrificed a lot for your family."

"Some may see it like that, but to me, it wasn't a sacrifice. It was an opportunity to play the sport I loved, get an education, and learn about love. Tab and I are still friends, but we don't talk or see each other often."

"I love the dynamics of this family relationship. Everyone always seems so happy."

"We love what we do and the people who share our lives. I'd like if you were to become a part of that one day if you're ready."

"I'd like that very much," Luce said. She replaced the picture on the table. "I'm ready for a cold beer and a fantastic view if you are."

Cam walked into the kitchen and pulled out two beers, then reached for Luce's hand. "Come with me."

Cam opened a door that led to a small porch right off the water. She offered Luce a seat and a beer and sat beside her. She looked at her watch. "In about twenty minutes, you will see a fantastic sunset. The oranges and yellows of the last sunrays fade into the brown and green of the bayou. At certain times of the year, the sun sets behind that old cypress tree, and the orange glow brings the tree back to life."

Luce looked at Cam. "That was a beautiful description of the sunset and gave me a deeper perspective of the love you have for this place."

"This has been and always will be home. There's no place on earth I'd rather be."

"I understand and can feel it every time you speak of the bayou or your family."

Cam took a drink of her beer. "I had a great time with you today. Thanks for spending it with me."

"It was my pleasure. I enjoy being with you and learning so much about you and your family. I can't wait to go out with you tomorrow."

Cam grinned. "You realize we start at five in the morning. We can come back and get you later if you want."

"No, ma'am. I want every moment of the experience with you from start to finish."

"It's going to be a long day. We don't usually get home before dark."

"I work the mid-shift the next day, so I go in later. I'll sleep in that morning after you leave and head to work later in the day. If that works for you."

"That most definitely works for me."

Luce looked away from Cam to look across the bayou. "I see what you mean. The horizon lights up like it's on fire."

"Exactly," Cam said. "The morning is just as glorious as you'll find out tomorrow."

"I've seen it from my cruiser many times, but I'm sure it will be different on the water."

"It may start a bit cool on the water in the morning. We've got hoodies on the boat if you get cold."

"I've got a heavy long-sleeved T-shirt with me," Luce said.

"You can wear a Gator Girlz shirt over it, then take the long-sleeved one off once it starts warming up."

"Cool. I love those shirts. Does that make me an official Gator Girl?"

"If you hang with us all day, you'll have earned a T-shirt," Cam replied.

"That's a good deal. I look good in pink, too."

"Baby, you look good in anything," Cam told her and leaned over to kiss her.

"Thanks."

Cam's phone pinged with a text. She pulled out her phone. "Supper is ready." Cam drained her beer. "Are you ready?"

"I'm hungry," Luce said. "I've been thinking about lasagna all day."

"It's quite a treat when Wanda cooks it," Cam said.

"Let's go." Cam dropped the empty bottles in the trash.

Their hands instinctively joined as they walked across to the main house. As soon as they opened the door, the aroma of lasagna and garlic bread welcomed them. "Man, that smells good," Luce said to Wanda.

"Have a seat, and I'll bring the bread in just a minute."

"She's the only one in this house that doesn't burn the bread," Cam told Luce.

"Hey now, I've only burned it once, and that's because Wanda was distracting me," Liz replied.

"I'm terrible with bread, so they don't let me near the oven when it's cooking."

"Bread, yes, but when Mama passed, Cam took over the cooking and taught us many of her recipes," Wanda said. "She did such a good job that Cam lets us do most of the cooking inside."

"You're a natural in the kitchen, Wanda. Squirt and I are better with the grilling and the frying, so I'd say it was a fair trade."

Right on cue, Sandy came rushing in. "We're all set for a fire," she told Cam. "Let me wash up, and I'll be right there."

"It'll be a good night for the fire pit," Wanda said. "We might join you for a bit."

"The more, the merrier. We won't stay out late since we go back to work tomorrow."

Liz winked at Luce. "I hope you're ready for tomorrow. They may work ya hard."

"I don't mind hard work. I appreciate physical labor after sitting behind a steering wheel most of the day."

"You don't look like most of the other deputies with their donut bellies. If they had to chase an old woman down, I doubt most of them could do it," Wanda chuckled.

"We need to tighten up our physical requirements for sure," Luce said. "Granted, we don't have much excitement, but we need to be able to perform if a situation calls for physical intervention."

"I think Scott should make them work as volunteer firefighters now and then. Those guys stay in shape by keeping their equipment up," Wanda said with a chuckle.

"Or come gator hunting for a few days until they realize just how out of shape they are," Cam added.

Luce took a bite and moaned. "If I keep eating like this, I won't be able to chase down an old lady."

"No worries, we'll work it off you tomorrow," Sandy said as she slid into a chair beside Luce.

Luce smacked Sandy's knee. "Stop that."

It was the legend of Bubba Gump that enthralled Sandy. Her eyes were glued to Cam as she retold the story. The legendary gator that ruled the swamp had always captured her attention, and Sandy dreamed that one day she would be the hunter to finally bring down Bubba Gump and collect the ten-thousand-dollar bounty Hank had placed on him. Hank had been one of the last hunters to hook into Bubba Gump and the limp so evident when he walked was the reward of attempting to catch the beast. That had been the final year Hank hunted for gators, and his hatred of the creature grew with every painful step he took.

"That sounds like one mean gator," Luce said.

Cam nodded. "He is. You may get to see him for yourself tomorrow while we're out hunting. He's smart enough not to take our bait, but sometimes we catch a glimpse of him sunning or swimming in the sloughs."

"If you see a gator big as a tree with a red spot on the top of his head, that's him," Sandy added.

"Red spot?" Luce asked.

"Scars from being shot," Cam said. "Some say it's a bullseye to taunt hunters into going for him. Our daddy and Papi always warned us against going for the monster. He brings only bad things to those that hunt him."

"Sounds like one to leave alone," Luce said. "If he's been around for ages, he's not only mean, but smart to survive this long."

A dog howled in the distance sending an eerie chill down Sandy's spine. She drained the beer and looked at Cam. "I think I'm going to head off to bed. See you at five?"

"I've got the coffee pot set already," Cam said. "Get some rest so we can pull in a bunch of gators."

"I've got sausage and biscuits that just need to be warmed. Grab a bag before you leave tomorrow and pop it in the microwave to warm it. T and I will see you out on the water," Wanda told Squirt.

"Goodnight," Sandy said.

"Sleep well, Squirt," Cam called to her. "We should probably be heading in soon, too."

Wanda nodded at them. "Go ahead, and I'll kill the fire."

"Thanks again for another great meal," Luce told Wanda.

"My pleasure. See you in the morning."

"Goodnight," Cam told Liz and Wanda.

†

184

Sandy stripped down to her panties and a T-shirt before climbing into bed. Willow jumped to the end of the bed and circled three times before lying down in her usual spot. Amite had stretched out on her chest, softly purring as she turned out the light. "Goodnight, fur babies," she whispered and fell asleep stroking Amite's soft coat.

Cam and Luce stripped out of their clothes and climbed into bed. Their naked bodies entwined as they made love to the sounds of the bayou outside the window. When sated, Luce lay in Cam's arms, gently caressing her stomach with her fingertips. "Thank you for including me in your life. I had a fantastic time today, and I'm sure tomorrow will be another great adventure."

"Thank you for trusting in our love and being patient as we work through issues. I never meant to hurt you, and I promise to be honest with you moving forward. No secrets." Cam leaned over to kiss the top of Luce's head. She listened until Luce's breaths deepened, and she knew her lover had fallen asleep. Only minutes later, Cam's eyes closed, and she was down for the count.

†

Sandy woke with a start from a dream. She vaguely remembered that she was hunting Bubba Gump, but she did not recall what happened to startle her awake. A light sweat had broken out across her skin as Sandy dreamed, so it must have been vivid for her body to respond that way. She felt movement by her side and found Amite snuggled next to her. Sandy rolled over on her side and cuddled the kitten before drifting back to sleep.

†

Cam's eyes opened before the alarm went off, and she could smell the coffee brewing in the kitchen. She slipped quietly from the bed and dressed for work. Cam emptied the first pot of coffee into a thermos and made a smaller pot to fill mugs for the three of them. Cam returned to the bedroom and gently woke Luce with a kiss. "It's time to get to work."

"I'll be right up," Luce replied, and Cam walked to the bathroom to brush her teeth and hair. She secured her hair in a short ponytail and pulled it through the opening in the back of her cap.

"All set."

Luce was dressing as she exited the bathroom. "I put a T-shirt on the end of the bed for you. I'm going to get our coffee ready to go."

"I'm on my way. Let me pee and wash up quickly, and I'll meet you in the kitchen."

Cam stopped to kiss Luce on the lips. "Good morning. Welcome to gator hunting 101."

Luce smiled. "Thanks."

Cam poured three travel mugs with coffee and turned when she heard a soft tap on her door from Sandy, who peeked inside. "Come in. I've got your coffee ready."

"Thanks," Sandy replied as she took the mug. She handed Cam the bag of biscuits. "Do you want to warm these, and we can eat one before we go?"

"Sure. That sounds good to me." Cam opened the bag and took out three biscuits, and put them in the microwave.

"How do you feel this morning?"

"Revitalized and ready to haul in some gators."

Sandy nodded. "You look much more rested. Do you want us to bring in the first gator to demonstrate to Luce, and then she can take over the shooting?"

"That's good. Maybe if we hook something smaller, Luce can fight it to the boat." Cam grinned. "I know she's strong enough."

"I'd love to fight one, but only if you think I'm ready," Luce said as she pulled her hair into a ponytail.

"We'll see how the morning goes, but I'm sure you'll catch on quick," Cam said as she handed Luce coffee. "The biscuits are warm too."

Luce picked up the biscuit and took a bite. "Um, these are delicious."

"T made up a batch of egg salad that she'll drop off at the cabin for lunch," Sandy told them. "Karen made fresh cookies to send, too."

"Are we ready to go then?" Cam asked, eager to get on the water. She picked up a bunch of bananas and her coffee mug. Grab those biscuits for later." She looked at Luce. "Will you carry the thermos?"

"Absolutely."

"I've got the cooler stocked already," Sandy said as they walked to the door.

The sky was starting to lighten as they climbed aboard the airboat. Sandy loaded the rifle and ensured extra ammunition was in the console. She handed Cam her pistol and slipped hers into a shoulder rig. Luce watched with interest as they geared up.

"All set," Cam said.

Sandy handed out the ear mufflers and started the engine. The powerful fan that propelled the boat rippled the water as Sandy pulled from the slip and raced across the bayou to their first line.

"Down and tight," Sandy replied as the boat floated toward the line.

Cam reached for the rope with a gloved hand and began pulling. The incensed reptile thrashed in the water when he realized he was hooked and no longer in control, and the fight was on. Sandy picked up the rifle and moved closer to Cam as she battled the large gator.

Luce noticed how carefully Cam and Sandy maneuvered around the boat, staying clear of the rope on the floor and not allowing hands or feet to get tangled. After a long five-minute struggle, she heard Cam tell Sandy, "He's on his way up. Be ready on my right side."

Sandy moved closer to Cam but maintained enough distance to allow Cam to wrestle with the powerful animal. When Sandy saw the head emerge, she was lucky to have enough visibility and time to fire off a round before he resumed fighting.

"Great shot. Phew, that got my blood pumping," Cam said as she gave Sandy a high five. "Help me get him in the boat."

Luce paid attention to how they pulled the gator's head onto the side of the boat then wrapped the gator's snout with thick tape. Then with a heave, they moved the gator halfway out of the water. Sandy grabbed a back foot, and together they hauled the gator entirely in the boat.

"That thing is huge," Luce said, her eyes wide with surprise.

Sandy glanced at Cam. "Probably between ten and eleven feet, you reckon?"

"At least a good ten," Cam answered with a nod. "Let me reset the line, and we can move on." She removed her gloves and walked to the bait bucket.

Luce moved closer to watch what Cam was doing. She stepped back quickly when Cam opened the container of rancid chicken. "Dear God, what is that smell?"

"A feast for a hungry gator. We'd call it spoiled chicken." Cam ran the large hook through the meat and quickly rinsed her hands in the water. Sandy tossed her a clean towel.

Cam dried her hands and motioned Luce closer to the gator. "I know you were paying attention, but you have to be extremely careful not to get your hands or feet tangled in the rope when you're fighting a gator. One wrong move can cause some severe damage. Once we are sure the gator is dead, we tape his jaws shut, just in case we are wrong, and he's only stunned." She pointed out the entry of Sandy's shot. "The kill spot on a gator is only about the size of a half-dollar. Even then, with his thick skin, a good shot can ricochet, just stunning a gator. You always check for an oily stain in the water from the gator's blood."

Sandy agreed. "There's nothing more terrifying than an angry gator coming to life inside a small metal boat. Even with the jaws taped shut, the powerful tail and claws can do significant damage. Better to use a second bullet if there's any doubt."

Luce seemed impressed by their knowledge. "Are gators of this size pretty common?"

Cam nodded. "Yeah, he's relatively average size, so he's been smart enough to evade capture more than a few years. There are only so many gators we can take out of here in a thirty-day season. They reproduce faster than we can cull them. We try to get the biggest bulls, but for each one we take, there are plenty to take his place."

"I got tired just watching y'all, and you do this all day long?" Luce asked. "It's no wonder you're exhausted by the end of the day."

"We usually spend ten to twelve hours a day on the water, depending on the weather and how the gators are feeding," Sandy continued. "It's not easy work by any means."

"I can see that." Luce stood and walked to the cooler. She pulled out two bottles of Gatorade. "No time like the present to start hydrating."

Cam wiped the sweat from her brow and twisted the bottle open. She took a long drink and looked at Sandy. "I'll tag him if you want to drive to our next line."

Luce watched four more gators hauled into the boat. She wondered how many more before they would need to unload. "How many more before you head to LB's?"

"Probably one to two more," Sandy replied as they pulled up to a downed line.

Cam reached for the rope. It was tight, but she could tell it was a smaller gator. "You want to try this one?"

Luce swallowed hard. "Yeah, I think so."

Sandy tossed her a pair of gloves. "You'll need these."

Cam handed her the line and instructed her on how to pull the gator toward the boat. "Careful of the line and always be prepared for the gator to lunge erratically."

Cam stood close, and when the gator jumped to the left, Cam supported Luce to keep her stable. "Good job, wear him out," Cam praised her. "Sandy, are you ready?"

"Ready and waiting for him to pop his head out of the water." Sandy checked her load and got ready to aim for a quick shot.

The gator's head broke the surface, and Sandy fired. "Bam. One and done."

"Are you ready to pull him up?" Cam asked Luce.

"Sure." Luce grabbed the gator by the snout and pulled his head toward the boat. Sandy quickly wrapped the tape around his jaws, and then she and Luce brought the gator onboard.

"Wait," Cam said. She pulled out her phone. "Can you help her hold the gator's head up?" she asked Sandy. Sandy nodded and raised the head long enough for Luce to hold it and Cam to snap a picture. "Got it. Your first gator!"

"High five," Sandy said, and slapped palms with Luce.

"He's not as big as the others, but man, he was strong," Luce said.

"You did well," Cam praised. She looked at Sandy. "One more, and we drop them at LB's and grab an early lunch?"

"That sounds good to me. My biscuits are already gone." Sandy looked at Luce. "You up for shooting the next one?"

"Absolutely," Luce answered. She wiped her brow, and Cam thought she looked adorable in her gator hunting outfit.

The next gator was the biggest of the day. When Cam finally got him close enough for a shot, Luce missed the first time but quickly took a second shot, landing perfectly in the kill zone.

"This old boy has been around a long time," Cam said as she muscled his head out of the water. "Will you wrap him?"

Luce quickly wrapped the heavy tape around his jaws, then helped Cam pull him into the boat. "Twelve feet?" she asked Cam.

"If not, just a hair shy. This gator is almost as long as the boat." Cam took a seat beside Luce.

Sandy turned the airboat and drove across the bayou as fast as she dared with such a heavy load. When she floated into the loading zone at LB's, Hank was standing there waiting on them.

"Well, I'll be. You breaking in another Gator Girl, Cam?"

"Yes, sir, and I have to admit she did pretty well on her first gator."

"I think I'm going to feel it in every muscle in my body tomorrow, too," Luce replied.

"It will keep you in great shape like these two. I'd hate to tangle with any of the St. Angelo sisters." Hank chuckled.

"This last one is a big boy," Sandy said. "The boys will need the winch for him."

"Are the gators biting good today?" Hank asked Sandy.

Sandy grinned up at him. "One on every line so far, and we've just started the run. If this holds up, you may see us several times today."

"Have T and Wanda made it in yet?" Cam asked.

"Nope. I do believe they are on the way." Hank pointed at an approaching boat.

"Great timing. Let's get unloaded and head back for a sandwich. Or two," Cam said.

"You heard the ladies, boys, get to unloading," Hank barked.

Wanda pulled up behind them, and Cam saw an excellent load of gators. "Looking good."

"A few smaller ones, but most are decent sized. We've got nine on this load." T looked up at Cam. "I think the day off was good for the gators, too. We've hit on every line so far."

"Same here. Today is going to be a multiple trip day," Cam replied.

"You gals still interested in some extra tags?" Hank asked.

"Ask us again when we get close to tagging out, but probably so," Cam said. "At this rate, we'll top three hundred today."

"Easily, you're almost there with these two loads. Two more loads each, and you'll be well on your way. Chance has had a string of bad luck with boat motors and his help bailing on him. If you could pick up fifteen to twenty-five, I know he'd appreciate the help."

"I don't see a problem with it, but don't jinx us yet," Cam teased.

"All right, ladies, it looks like you're good to go. Hurry back."

"Will do, Hank," Sandy said.

"Meet us at the cabin for sandwiches," Cam called to Wanda.

Wanda shot her a thumb's up as Sandy's engine roared to life.

Sandy pulled out of the loading slip then raced for the island. Cam stepped onto the dock and tied them off. She reached for Luce's hand as Sandy jumped onto the boardwalk.

"Show off," Luce grinned at Sandy.

"Younger and faster. Probably hungrier, too," Sandy replied and walked ahead of them.

"Let's wash up and get to fixin' some sandwiches. I hope you like egg salad. If not, there may be some bologna left."

"I love egg salad," Luce answered.

Sandy washed up in the kitchen while Cam showed Luce the bathroom, and they washed up and shared a quick kiss before heading back into the kitchen.

Sandy had bread slices scattered across the table on paper towels and was busy making sandwiches. "You must be hungry," Cam replied.

"Yeah, and I want to get back out on the water, too, so we can maybe get two more loads in." Sandy grinned.

"Such a slave driver," Cam teased. "What do y'all want to drink?" Cam opened the refrigerator. "Tea, sodas, water, and milk."

"Tea is fine with me," Luce said.

"Me too," Sandy echoed.

Cam was pouring tea and bringing it to the table when she heard Wanda's motor approaching. She stepped out and hollered, "Whatcha drinking?"

"Tea," they both replied.

Cam stepped back inside, made two more tea glasses, and placed the container on the table.

T and Wanda stomped their boots to remove any dirt and stepped into the cabin. "Now this is service," T said.

"Wash up, and let's eat," Cam told them.

Sandy took a bite of a sandwich and moaned. "This tastes great," she said after swallowing.

"There was lasagna left if y'all want to come over for leftovers tonight," Wanda said.

"That sounds good to me," Luce replied. "I have a feeling I'll be starving by the end of the day."

Cam nodded. "Yes, you will. That's a guarantee."

Wanda picked up a sandwich. "Hank says we're up to two ninety-nine with this morning's load."

Sandy gave Cam a high five. "Killing it."

"Do you think you can bring in two more loads today?" Cam asked.

"I think that's very doable." Wanda looked at T, who nodded.

"I told Hank we'd help Chance out with some of his tags, but we had to finish ours first."

"At this rate, we could tag out this weekend." T grinned. "The extra income would be a nice bonus."

"That's what we thought, too," Sandy replied. She picked up a second sandwich.

"How did our newest Gator Girl do?" Wanda asked.

Cam pulled out her phone and showed Wanda and T the photo she had snapped of Luce and her first gator. "She was impressive."

"He was smaller than the rest, but I'm still proud," Luce said. "I wouldn't mind helping out on my off days until y'all get done this season."

"Ya picked a good one," Wanda said with a wink to Cam.

Cam picked up another sandwich. "If we finish by Friday, we can take the weekend off and pick up the new tags Monday. Running two boats, I think we can knock out thirty tags before the season's over."

"Without a doubt," Wanda replied.

Sandy finished her sandwich and started to pick up the table. "Someone's excited," T said.

"She's been a ball of energy all day," Cam said. "Go on out. We'll be there in a minute."

"I think the day off helped us all," T said. "It sure was nice to sleep through a sunrise for a change."

Cam nodded. "Yes, it was. Y'all need to let me know when you need a break."

Wanda smirked. "Now she tells us when the season's almost over."

"You can tell me anytime you need a break. We're only human," Cam said and looked at her sisters. "Even the great Cam St. Angelo gets worn out."

Laughter broke out around the table. "I gotta get rid of some tea," she said. "Go, Sandy. I'll be there in a minute."

Sandy rushed outside and was waiting in the boat when Cam and Luce returned. "All set?" she asked after they took their seats. She started the engine before Cam could reply, and had them heading toward the lines at top speed.

Cam looked at Luce, smiled, and shook her head.

†

Their first line still had bait hanging. Sandy was disappointed but wasn't worried until the following line was also untouched. "What do you think is going on?"

Cam searched the area until her eyes spotted a large creature sunning on the bank of the slough fifty yards ahead. She pointed. "That's what's going on. Bubba Gump has claimed this spot for himself, and no other gator will enter this slough with him here."

"Or get eaten," Sandy added.

"Hot damn, that's a big gator," Luce said.

Cam looked at Sandy. "We might as well leave this slough for today. Ain't nothing gonna be biting here."

"We've got plenty other lines set. It just pisses me off that Bubba Gump disturbed the flow we had going," Sandy said, then spun the boat around.

Sandy anxiously pulled up to the start of the next set of lines and breathed a sigh of relief when the line was down and tight. "You two have this?"

"Yes, we're good." Cam slid her gloves over her hands and reached for the rope. "Oh, he's a good one," Cam called out.

"Bring him on in, Cam." Sandy couldn't remain in her seat and walked to where Cam was fighting the gator. "Let me know if you need a rest. He looks to be fighting hard."

Cam nodded. "He is, but I'm not letting this big boy get away from me."

Sandy watched Cam fight the gator for almost a full five minutes before he began tiring, and she could pull him closer to the boat. "I think he's finally coming," Cam said through gritted teeth.

When Luce saw the water ripple and the gator's head appear, she fired quickly.

"Great shot," Sandy told her. She waited until Cam brought the gator head onto the boat for taping. "Let me spell ya on this one, sis."

"I won't argue with you. That gator was an ass-kicker." Cam waited until Sandy had a firm hold on the gator's head before stepping away. She plopped into a seat and wiped her face and arms with a towel. "Damn."

Sandy grinned over at Luce. "You ready to haul this big boy into the boat?"

Luce grabbed a front leg, and they managed to get his front half in the boat.

Cam warned Luce. "He's a long one, so be careful of that tail when he gets on board. The weight of it alone can knock ya over."

It took several attempts, but Sandy and Luce finally brought the gator on board. "What a beast," Sandy declared and walked to the cooler for a cold drink. She handed one to Luce and Cam. "It's starting to heat up out here. Drink up."

Luce took a long drink and then removed the long-sleeved shirt, leaving only the Gator Girlz T-shirt. "That's better already."

"Get moving so we can get a bit of air before the next line," Cam requested.

Sandy walked to the driver's seat. "I've got the next one. You take a break."

Cam nodded and took another long drink. She admitted to herself that the fight in that gator took a toll on her. Cam lifted her face to the breeze as Sandy drove farther into the slough.

When they approached the following line, Sandy turned off the engine and handed Cam a banana as she passed by. "This will help."

"Thanks," Cam said and peeled the banana. She took a bite as she watched Sandy secure the line. "He feel like a good one?"

"He ain't no baby," Sandy said as she reached down to clear a broken limb from the line. The gator sensed the movement and lunged toward the boat.

Luce, startled by the aggressive movement, let out a yelp. "Madder than a hatter."

Sandy nodded and began wrestling the gator closer to the boat. When the gator's head popped up, Luce aimed and pulled the trigger. "Click" was all they heard.

"Damn. Out of bullets," Luce said.

Cam raced to hand her a box of shells. "You okay, Squirt?"

"I'm good," Sandy replied.

Luce reloaded the rifle and took a shot. "Sorry, I should have double-checked the magazine. I'll reload when we get this one in the boat."

"No harm, no foul. We have all made the same mistake," Sandy said. "You ready?"

"Yeah, bring him up." Luce planted a shot squarely in the kill spot and turned to store the rifle.

Cam still held the box of shells. "Give it to me, and I'll reload while y'all tag that beast."

Luce handed her the rifle and returned to help Sandy. "Do you carry salt tablets?" she whispered.

"Yeah, we do." Sandy's head spun around to look at Cam. Her shirt soaked with sweat clung to her body. "I'll pass some out before we move on."

"Thanks," Luce replied. "Ready?"

"Let's do this," Sandy chuckled.

Sandy opened the console and removed salt tablets, and handed them out. "We all need these today."

"Yeah, we do," Cam agreed. "Ready to move on?"

Sandy nodded and started the engine. After four more lines, they had six large gators, and the boat was riding significantly lower in the water. "I think we need to offload before we sink," she told Cam.

"Amen to that. I'm not ready to swim home."

Sandy turned the boat and drove fast enough to generate a cool breeze. She worried about Cam. The day off had been good for all of them, but Cam still didn't appear one hundred percent. Sandy hoped the last load of the day would go quickly, and they could head for home before dark.

Hank spotted them coming in and came out holding more cold Sun Drops. "Y'all look like you could use these," he said as he passed them out.

Sandy accepted the drink. "It's a burner out here today for sure. We got some nice ones on this load. Damn, Bubba Gump ran everything out of one of our sloughs today."

"I don't think that old bastard is ever going to die off," Hank said.

"One day, he'll meet his maker," Sandy said.

"Are you going to shoot for one more load or call it a day?" Hank asked. "You're well over three hundred with what T and Wanda will bring in."

"I've promised them a weekend off if we can tag out by Friday," Cam said. "I think we've got one more load in us today."

"Let's get ya unloaded then and back on your way. Chance is delighted that y'all have agreed to help him with some tags."

"He'd do the same for us, Hank, if we needed it," Cam answered.

"Yeah, he would. I'll see you when y'all come back in. How about a cold Abita before you head home?"

"Sounds great," Sandy said and reached into her pocket.

"Slow ya roll, Missy. These are on me," Hank laughed.

"Makes 'em taste even better when someone else buys," Cam said with a smile.

"They will be ice cold and ready when you get back," Hank promised.

†

Two hours later, they pulled into LB's with another full load of eleven gators. Sandy pointed out that T and Wanda were on their way in as well.

"Good timing," Sandy called to Wanda when she pulled up behind them.

Wanda wiped her hand across her face. "What a day."

"Looks like you've got a full load, too," Cam said.

"Sixteen." T grinned. "Not all the biggest, but none under nine feet."

"That's still a great day," Cam replied.

Hank started handing out beer. "How many did you say? Did I hear sixteen?"

"Yes, sir, you heard correctly," T answered.

"That gives you three twenty-two in total. One more day, and y'all should tag out and get a three-day weekend." Hank looked at Cam. "If the boss agrees."

"I think we've earned it," Cam told him.

Sandy tapped her bottle to Cam's. "Here's to a three-day weekend."

"Hear, hear," the rest of the group chimed in.

They ended up sharing a second beer with Hank before heading home. Sandy pulled out first and couldn't resist taking a wide turn and spraying Wanda and T as they left LB's before racing home.

"You know you're going to pay for that, right?" Cam teased her. "I don't know when, how, or where, but Wanda will get payback."

"I know, but right now, it was worth it," Sandy said as she pulled into the boat slip.

"I think we're going to clean up and stretch out for a bit," Cam said. "See you for leftovers at seven?"

"Sounds good, if I'm still able after Wanda gets her hands on me," Sandy laughed.

"You laugh now, but I bet she gets the last laugh. We'll see you later. I hope," Cam added with a smirk. She reached for Luce's hand, and they walked home.

"Will Wanda do something devious to Sandy?" Luce asked.

"You never know about a St. Angelo," Cam warned with a grin.

†

After dinner, Cam and Luce headed home to crash onto the bed. They were both exhausted and ready for sleep after eating their fill. Wanda exacted Sandy's revenge by waiting until she got in the shower and lathered before cutting off the hot water. Wanda was surprised Cam and Luce didn't hear Sandy yelling when the ice-cold water hit her.

"I'm glad you decided to start at six tomorrow. It shouldn't take long for y'all to tag out the way things were rolling today," Luce said as she snuggled into Cam.

Cam ran her hand over Luce's bare shoulder. "We'll probably finish midafternoon at the latest. We'll go ahead and pull our lines and not leave them up over the weekend. That makes anything caught easy prey for predators like Bubba Gump and at risk of drowning."

"I've never seen a gator that big," Luce told Cam.

"He's da demon of da bayou," Cam said.

"I work until eleven tomorrow. Will you call me when you get home and shower?"

"Yes, ma'am, I will. Will you have breakfast with me in the morning?"

"I'll cook while you get ready for work," Luce said.

"Perfect," Cam kissed the top of her head. "Thanks for spending the day with us on the water. You were impressive."

"I have tremendous respect for what y'all do now. I had no idea how physically draining that work can be, but I do now. The small amount I did will have me sore as heck tomorrow."

"You get used to it after a while," Cam answered. "You still get tired, but the soreness wears off the next morning."

"I think I'll feel it long after the morning," Luce replied. "I have a hard time keeping my eyes open."

"Snuggle in then, and we'll get some sleep. Goodnight, Luce," Cam whispered.

†

Luce climbed from the bed the following day and slipped on a clean T-shirt. She walked into the kitchen and was preparing breakfast when Cam walked into the room.

"Good morning." Cam wrapped her arms around Luce and kissed her neck. "I thought I smelled bacon. Let me get dressed, and I'll be right back."

Luce dropped the bread in the toaster as she finished frying eggs for Cam. She slid them onto a plate with a handful of bacon, and buttered the toast. Luce poured two large glasses of juice and a mug of coffee. Luce cracked her eggs to cook while she placed Cam's breakfast on the table.

"Wow, that looks great," Cam said when she returned. "How do you feel this morning?"

"A little sore but not as bad as I feared. This juice will help. I hope," Luce answered. Her toast was ready, so she slid her eggs onto a plate and joined Cam.

Cam dabbed up the final bit of yolk with her toast. "You can cook me breakfast anytime."

Luce smiled. "I'm glad you enjoyed it." Luce looked at the time. "Sandy will be here any minute. Do you need drinks or anything for today?"

"I'm sure she's stocked us already. She's probably been up since five. I'll clean up and head out to meet her."

"Go, and I'll clean up before I head back to town. I've got plenty of time to kill before I go to work."

"Thanks again for a delicious breakfast and a few great days together. When can we get together again?"

"I have it from a reliable source that you have a long weekend coming up. I work the early shifts. I could come out after work. Someone still owes me a steak dinner."

"I have not forgotten," Cam told her. "Is Friday or Saturday better for you? I think the shrimp will be here Saturday morning."

"Steaks on Saturday. Maybe I'll bring some pizzas out on Friday. Give everyone a break from cooking."

"Pizza, tomorrow night sounds great. I'll let the others know."

"Great." Luce leaned in for a kiss. "Be careful and remember to drink today. I worry about you."

"Cross my heart. I'll talk to you tonight."

†

Sandy was pacing the boardwalk, waiting on Cam. She had been awake since four when another dream of Bubba

Gump woke her, and she couldn't fall back asleep. Sandy finally got up and made French toast and bacon for herself, Wanda, and Liz, who worked the midshift at the hospital today.

Sandy smiled when she heard Cam's door open and saw her sister walk onto the porch, then stop for a final kiss from Luce. Luce was great for Cam, and Sandy was delighted to see Cam falling in love again.

"Let's go, Romeo," she called to Cam as she walked across the yard.

"I'm coming. Just hold your horses."

Cam stepped on board and took a sip of coffee. "You ready to tag out today?"

"I'm always ready to hear that last tag click," Sandy said.

CHAPTER NINE

Sandy and Cam worked hard filling tags and pulling up lines. At one, they delivered a second load to LB's. Hank handed Cam the extra tags.

"I didn't know if you wanted these today in case you needed a few for the gators y'all caught today," Hank said.

Cam took the tags and stored them. "Let's see if T and Wanda have finished for the day or if we need to hit the lines again today, if you're up for it, that is," Cam teased.

"Silly question," Sandy grinned. "Let's go."

T and Wanda were on their way in when Sandy pulled out. They had brought in enough gators to fill their last tags. "Let's go crack open some cold ones," Cam said.

"We'll be right behind you," Wanda said and drove the boat toward LB's.

Sandy was halfway across the bayou when she spotted a large gator two hundred yards away on the water. She pointed him out to Cam. "Do you want me to take a chance of sniping him?"

"He looks huge," Cam replied.

Sandy killed the engine and scampered down from the driver's seat to pull out her deer rifle with a powerful scope. The boat continued to drift, and Cam slid over to the driver's seat to guide it toward the gator. Sandy lifted the gun and brought the gator into her sights. When she spotted the red dot on the gator's head, she swallowed hard. Maybe this was why she had dreamed of Bubba Gump for the last two nights. The dreams could be an omen, now was her time.

"That's not just a big gator. It's Bubba Gump." Sandy looked at Cam, and she was wearing a strange expression.

"I know you're grown and can make up your mind, but I don't like this. Do you wanna try? I'm with you if you want to take a crack at him, but Bubba Gump scares me."

"Yeah, Cam, I do. I've dreamed of Bubba Gump the last two nights. Maybe it was an omen that now is my time."

"Be careful then. You know Bubba's a mean sumbitch," Cam warned.

Sandy nodded, fully aware of the legend behind the massive gator and the injuries he had caused over the years. Most hunters would drive away, but Sandy had always dreamed she'd be the hunter to bring Bubba Gump down. "It's an almost impossible shot from this distance, but I wanna try."

Cam nodded and watched as Sandy lifted her rifle.

Sandy took a deep breath and located Bubba in her sights. The legendary gator was swimming right toward them, daring Sandy to take a shot. She let out her breath slowly as her finger moved to the trigger and squeezed off a shot. Sandy's eyes grew wide as she watched the gator roll several times, churning up the water, and then fell silent. "I got him, Cam. I really got him. Come on, let's go get him."

Cam cried out. "I can't believe you made the shot, but I watched him roll and then die down." She drove the boat closer, knowing they only had minutes before he would sink to the bottom of the bayou and be gone forever.

Sandy saw the bloody oil stain surrounding the gator and tossed the treble hook out to pull him to the boat.

"Holy shit, you got him," Cam said as she joined Sandy.

"Yeah, I did," Sandy said, and she began reaching down to grab his head.

"Hang on and let me put another in him just to make sure," Cam said and pulled out her pistol. She was aiming for the sweet spot and had squeezed the trigger when she saw Bubba Gump's eyes flash open as he lunged for Sandy. Cam's shot was accurate but fractions of a second too late. Bubba Gump's front teeth had raked down the inside of Sandy's left arm. Her baby sister was screaming in agony as she held the shredded remains of her left arm against her body.

Sandy saw the blood and began to feel faint. Her arm was bleeding badly, but she didn't see a gush indicating an artery was affected. Cam froze for a few seconds and then rushed into action, wrapping a towel around her arm. "Hold it tight to slow the bleeding until I can get us out of here."

Sandy watched the towel stain red as Cam called Bren to get an ambulance to LB's. Sandy's eyes turned to Bubba Gump, now floating beside the boat, matching it in length. "We can't leave him, Cam."

"The hell we can't," Cam growled.

"Please, Cam, tie a rope around him. I can't bear the thought of the pain I'm going to endure only to watch him sink to the bottom of the bayou. Please," she begged.

Cam worked quickly to get a rope around him and tie him off to the boat. "Now, we're going." Cam started the engine, and the weight of the gator pulled hard against the boat. Cam was frustrated with the slow progress, but Sandy was determined to deliver Bubba to Hank. She breathed a sigh of relief when she saw T and Wanda headed her way. She slowed long enough to toss the rope to Wanda. "Sandy got Bubba, but he got her. Take him in and meet us at the hospital."

With the weight of the gator gone, Cam drove at full speed to LB's.

Sandy had lost color in her face, and she looked on the verge of fainting. "I got him, Cam."

"Yeah, you did, Squirt."

Tony and several of the men from LB's jumped on board and helped the EMTs get Sandy onto a stretcher and prepped to go to the hospital. Cam rode in the ambulance with Sandy but had to wait outside the exam room while the medical staff attended to Sandy's injuries.

"I'll be all right, Cam," was the last thing she heard before she slid down the wall in shock.

An off-duty fireman recognized Cam and got her seated in a chair, sipping cool water. Liz rushed down the hall, took one look at Cam, and entered the exam room.

Sandy looked at the blurry faces surrounding her, but she forced a smile when she heard Liz's voice. "Hey, sis. I got Bubba Gump."

"That's great, Squirt, but right now, we need to get you patched up."

"Okay," Sandy replied, delirious from the blood loss, and lost consciousness.

Liz's eyes shot to the monitors. Sandy's vitals were strong, but her blood pressure was low. Liz stepped into the hall and walked to Cam. "We're going to need some of that rare St. Angelo blood. I assume the sisters are coming?"

"Yeah," Cam replied.

"Go to the blood bank as soon as you can and get to pumping. Sandy's going to need at least four pints, during and after surgery."

"On it," Cam replied.

†

Sandy felt like she was floating. The darkness surrounding her was as deep as the bayou at midnight. She felt no pain, which she found odd since her arm was severely damaged. *I wonder if I'm dying? Or already dead? Don't people report seeing their lives flash before their eyes when they were dying? That isn't what is happening to me, but it feels so strange yet comforting.*

Sandy felt a shift in the room, and she opened her eyes. The most beautiful woman with blond hair and sparkling green eyes sat next to her examining her wounds. Liz stood next to her. "Have I died and gone to heaven?" she asked. "She's beautiful."

"Doc Vincent, meet Sandy St. Angelo," Liz said.

Maggie Vincent looked at Sandy. "It's great to meet you. You've done a number on this arm, and I'll be taking you to surgery in a few minutes. When you feel better, I need to hear the story of how this happened. The whole hospital is buzzing with news of you and Bubba Gump. No clue who he

210

is, but it sounds exciting. Relax, and I'll do my best to get you all patched up."

Sandy felt the warmth in the woman's eyes, and the softness of her voice made her body thrum with excitement. "Okay, Doc." Sandy felt her eyes fading shut as she heard the doctor say, "Get her to room one, as quickly as possible." Her voice faded, and the blackness returned.

†

Sandy woke to the sound of crying. Her eyes would not open, but she felt a strong hand holding hers. She moved her fingers, and the crying stopped suddenly, and she heard Cam's voice.

"Sandy, I hope you will forgive me. I should have known better than to let you go after Bubba. I knew it deep in my gut, but I didn't stop you, and now look at what happened. I am so sorry for allowing you to be hurt. I wish it were me in this bed rather than you."

Sandy's eyes were still not cooperating, and her lips would not budge. Her fingers still worked, and she squeezed Cam's hand as hard as she could. Sandy could never remember seeing Cam cry, even though she knew she did when Mama and Dad died, and when Tab and she broke up. Never, ever in front of her sisters, though. She had always been their rock, the strongest to hold them all together in good times and bad. Hearing the pain in Cam's voice unsettled her, and she wished she could speak to Cam to ease her agony.

†

When Sandy finally opened her eyes, Doc Vincent was sitting beside her bed, examining her arm. Her green eyes were still brilliant, but she looked tired. Sandy opened her mouth, and a croak of a voice said, "You look tired."

Doc Vincent looked at Sandy. "It took me well into the morning to get you all patched up. I stayed here last night, just in case you needed me. Can you handle a sip of water?"

Sandy nodded and took a straw into her mouth. The cool water soaked in like raindrops in the desert. "Thank you," she whispered.

"Your throat is probably on fire from the breathing tube you had during surgery. We took it out as soon as possible, but it will be sore for a day or two. How do you feel?"

"Like I have been through a meat grinder. I can't lift my arm," Sandy frowned.

"We have you immobilized. I can't have you thrashing around in bed fighting gators and ruining all my hard work." The doctor smiled sweetly at her. "I won't lie to you. You have a difficult road to recovery ahead, but from what I hear of the St. Angelos, you will do just fine. You also had the best surgeon for miles working on your arm." She winked at Sandy.

Sandy's heart melted every time the woman spoke to her, but she knew she had to talk to Cam. "Is Cam here?"

"She hasn't left the hospital since you arrived. Even that good-looking deputy couldn't drag her out."

Sandy cracked a smile. "Her girlfriend, Luce. Can I see Cam?"

Maggie nodded. "Only a few minutes, you need to rest. I'll send her in."

"Thanks. Hey, Doc?"

"Yes?"

"Thank you for everything. I hope you sleep now."

"I will. See you later today."

Sandy watched her leave and was smiling when Cam entered the room moments later. "Hey," she whispered.

Cam sat beside her, and Sandy could see the tears in her eyes. "You look like crap. Go home and rest."

"I didn't want to leave you."

"I'm going to be okay, Cam. I heard what you said, and what happened was not your fault. It was my ego that made the decision, and I've learned that lesson the hard way. I'm in good hands here, so please let Luce take you home and get some sleep."

"I should have stopped you," Cam insisted.

"No, I was determined it was my time. I've been dreaming of Bubba Gump for days, and I thought it was an omen that it was my opportunity to bring him down." She laughed, then grimaced from the pain in her arm. "I was partly right. I've got a beautiful doctor and great nurses taking care of me, so please get some rest. I need you strong for when I come home."

Cam nodded. "Now that I see you're doing better, I will. Luce has taken the day off."

"Good, so go home and relax. I'll be fine. Liz snuck in earlier, so I know she'll be back."

"I'll be back this evening then. Anything you want?"

"T-shirt and shorts to sleep in and some Sun Drop," Sandy replied. "These hospital gowns are not flattering, and I've got a beautiful Doc to impress."

"She is gorgeous, and according to Liz, available," Cam replied.

"I'm way out of my league with this one, but it's nice flirting with her."

"If you can catch Bubba Gump and survive, catching a green-eyed doc should be a piece of cake for you." Cam's smile faded. "Hank's pretty torn up bout you getting hurt, blaming himself for that damned bounty."

"I would have tried for him even without the temptation of the bounty. Please let him know I'm okay and will see him when I get moved to a regular room."

"I will. Love you, Squirt."

"More. Now get, so I can sleep and dream of a beautiful woman," Sandy teased.

"See ya later, then."

"Bye, Cam."

Sandy's arm was throbbing. She picked up the button for the pain medication pump and pushed it. Within a minute, she felt the medicine entering her system, and her eyes were too heavy to stay open.

Her fighting spirit, love, and support from family and friends helped Sandy regain her strength and return home in record time. Hank insisted on paying for her medical bills and planned a mounting presentation to display Bubba Gump at the processing plant. Hank would probably go to his grave feeling guilty, but Sandy did her best to convince him that it was her decision and hers alone.

Liz performed wound care in the following weeks, and Maggie began making house calls to check on her star patient. There was an undeniable spark between them that grew into a budding romance. When Maggie had cleared Sandy to begin physical therapy, it began at the hospital. Sandy argued for home therapy, but Maggie insisted she come to the hospital so she could more closely monitor her progress. Sandy had already begun to realize she couldn't say "no" to Maggie so she relented on the location of therapy.

One afternoon when Maggie was making a house call, she examined Sandy's arm and smiled. "Your arm is progressing well. You know, you never did tell me the story of Bubba Gump. I mean, I know the end result, but tell me your story with him, please."

Sandy walked to the refrigerator and grabbed two Sun Drops, and reached for Maggie's hand. "Come with me."

Maggie took her hand and reached for the bottles. "Let me have those, please."

Sandy led them out to the pavilion and they took a seat looking across the water. Maggie opened their bottles and Sandy took a sip.

"The St. Angelo family has been on this property for over two hundred years. I believe a bit of the swamp water runs through our veins, and the love of this bayou rests deep in our hearts. Every one of us has had an opportunity to leave, but the bayou draws us back." Sandy took a sip of drink and continued. "Cam was the first to leave, to attend LSU and play softball, but she returned home when our mama, Camille, took sick. Our daddy, Ronny, needed Cam's help with Mama and in raising us four girls. Without a moment's hesitation, Cam left school to come home. After Mama passed away and the business was holding steady, Cam returned for one final year of college and softball. She had always dreamed of playing in the College World Series in Oklahoma City and she achieved that dream. The team didn't win, but Cam did her best. It was also the final time she had with Tab, her first love, who went on to law school at Duke. Tab would have loved for Cam to go with her, but she knows Cam's heart rests right here," Sandy said as her eyes scanned the bayou.

"That had to be tough for Cam," Maggie said.

"It was, but Cam buckled down and the business grew under her leadership when Daddy died. Karen and Teresa, who we call T, fell in love with two brothers, Jeff and Buster, and married shortly after they graduated. Those are their homes, and their husbands both work offshore," Sandy said, pointing out two of the houses on the homestead. "Karen has two boys who we all raise as ours." Sandy paused for a few seconds. "Wanda was nearly as good on the softball diamond as Cam, but she passed on playing ball to finish a business degree in three years. She handles most of the bookkeeping duties for Gator Girlz, Inc. Wanda twisted her ankle playing with the boys one day and that's when she met Liz. Liz will say Wanda turned on her irresistible St. Angelo charm, and there was no going back. Wanda makes it sound like she worked hard to win Liz's favor, but we all know better."

Maggie smiled. "Then there is you. Squirt, Sandy, and now people are calling you Little Tiger."

"Yes, then there's me. The baby sister. The runt of the litter."

"Did you ever think about college?"

"Not even for a second when Coach teased me with a full ride. I've no desire to leave the bayou, and all I need to know the bayou and my family teaches me."

"You have a very unique and special family."

"I wouldn't trade them for anything in this world."

"So, tell me about Bubba Gump."

"Ever since we were little, we were told stories about the demon of the bayou, a huge gator with a large red scar from being shot many times by hunters. We were taught to respect him when he was in our hunting area and warned about how mean he was."

"So, why did you want to catch him?"

"Hunters who attempted to catch Bubba for years, several, including Hank, were injured during the attempt. My ego outweighed my brain when it came to Bubba. I knew deep in my gut, that trying for him was a huge mistake, but the little devil of ego on my shoulder kept saying *you got him*. I had dreams of Bubba the previous two nights, so my ego got the best of me." Sandy's hand instinctively touched her arm as she spoke. "Cam and I had just finished dropping a load of gators at LB's and were going to check some additional lines before the end of the day. Several minutes after we left, I spotted a huge gator swimming a couple hundred yards away. When I asked Cam if I should try to snipe it with my rifle, she was all for it. I left the driver's seat of the airboat and pulled out my rifle. When I brought the gator into my sights, I saw Bubba's distinctive red spot and my heart lodged in my throat." She took a sip of the drink.

"I looked back at Cam and told her it was Bubba. I swear the blood rushed from her face, but she told me it was my decision to make. I steadied my aim and took the shot. I'd hit him and he rolled several times and then went silent. It was incredible I could even hit him from that distance, but I had. I tucked my rifle away as Cam drove us closer. A dead gator will sink to the bottom quickly so I used a treble hook to pull him close enough to the boat so we could secure him. I remember thinking there's no way we could get him in the boat. He was way too big and as long as the airboat, so I reckoned we'd tie him to the boat and drag him to LB's." Sandy sighed. "I made the worst mistake of my life assuming Bubba was dead. The water around him was filled with bloody oil and he was not fighting as I pulled him close. Cam pulled out her pistol to add a security shot and just as she pulled her trigger, he lunged and his front teeth raked down my arm."

"Holy cow, that must have been terrifying."

"I was in shock when I saw the blood racing down my arm, drenching my cargo shorts. Luckily Cam sprang into action and wrapped a towel around my arm and called for an ambulance to meet us. The most terrifying thought that was going through my head was losing Bubba. I begged Cam to tie a rope around him and drag him in. I would have been shattered if we allowed him to sink to the bottom of the bayou."

"I can understand why that would hurt after all the pain and suffering you've gone through so far, and unfortunately it's far from over."

"At least I can smile every time I pull up to LB's and see that beast hanging on the side of his building."

"I will have to go see him for myself. The rumor at the hospital is that he was twenty feet long and weighed a ton."

Sandy laughed. "He's not quiet that big, but he's the biggest on record in these parts. I could have never caught him the traditional way on a bait line even if he wasn't too smart to bite. I'm strong, but my one hundred thirty pounds would have been no match for him."

Cam was pulling into sight. "Will you stay and eat dinner with us?" Sandy asked.

"I would love to, but I have surgery in the morning, so I can't stay late," Maggie replied.

"No problem. We'll get you fed and on your way home before it gets late."

Sandy turned around when the door opened and Wanda stepped outside. "I set an extra plate, so you two come inside and clean up."

"See, we all think alike." Sandy smiled and dumped their empty bottles. When she turned back to Maggie, she was holding her hand out. Sandy slipped her hand inside Maggie's and they entered the house.

After dinner, Sandy walked Maggie out to her car. "Thanks for spending the afternoon with me and having dinner with us."

"It was my pleasure. I enjoyed getting to know you and your family a little more. Thank you, for sharing your story and your family with me.

Sandy was taken by surprise when Maggie leaned in and kissed her. It was more than a chaste kiss, and left her motionless for several long seconds.

Maggie's eyes searched hers. "I hope I wasn't wrong for doing that."

Sandy's speech returned. "I've wanted that kiss since I first met you at the hospital."

"I will be discharging you as a patient soon, but I'd like to get to know you better. Would you join me for dinner tomorrow night?" Maggie asked.

"When and where?" Sandy asked eagerly.

"You still need high doses of protein. How about the best steak in town, at six?"

Sandy laughed. "It's the only steak place in town, but that'll work fine with me. I'll sweet-talk Cam into cooking steaks for us one night. That's truly the best steak in town."

"That sounds delicious. See you at six?" Maggie climbed into her car and Sandy closed the door behind her.

"Yes, ma'am, I'll be there."

"Goodnight, Little Tiger," Maggie winked.

"Night, Doc, drive safe."

Sandy watched Maggie's tail lights fade into the night. "Hot damn!" Her feet barely touched the ground as she walked back toward the house. She laughed to herself when she saw the blinds in the living room moving and knew her sisters had been spying on her.

"Well?" Wanda said.

"Well, what?" Sandy played innocent.

"Did you ask her out?"

"Nope."

"No? Why the hell not?" Liz growled.

"Didn't have to, Maggie asked me first. We're going to dinner tomorrow night," Sandy smiled. "Oh shit."

"What?" Liz said.

"We are going for steak." Sandy raised her bandaged arm.

"You can do one of two things," Liz said. "Ask the kitchen to cut the steak for you before serving, or allow Maggie to help you. There's nothing weak about asking for help when you're vulnerable. Maggie may suggest it beforehand."

Sandy turned to Wanda. "Speaking of help. Will you iron me an outfit?"

"You will be creased and starched to impress," Wanda promised her.

†

Sandy was nervous as she pulled up to the steakhouse. Wanda had raved about how handsome she looked before she left, but Sandy's nerves were a bit on edge.

Maggie had already arrived and waved her over to the table. "You know I wasn't thinking clearly when I chose this place last night. I know it will be difficult for you to cut a steak. Would you be embarrassed if I cut it for you? We could also ask the server to have it cut."

Sandy laughed. "I was a bit worried about that too. Let's ask the cook to cut it and that way we can enjoy the meal together. I'm not embarrassed though, but I didn't want you to think I wouldn't ask for help. I can be a bit stubborn at times."

"Really?" Maggie teased. "I would have never guessed. Let's order, I'm starved."

As they waited for their meals to arrive, Maggie shared how she became a doctor and her love for helping people resume a normal life after major traumas. Her family was in the Houma area, but they weren't a close family. Sandy thought it was strange how families could drift so far apart, but it was more common these days than in the past.

When they left the restaurant that evening, Maggie turned to Sandy. "I had a lovely time with you tonight, and there's nothing more than I'd like to do than to take you home with me and spend all night exploring you."

"But?" Sandy said.

"You still need time to heal and I'm enjoying getting to know you. I don't want to rush into a physical relationship."

"I understand completely, so don't worry. I don't plan on going anywhere." Sandy smiled. "I think we'll both know when the time is right."

"Thank you for understanding. Some people would just dive in and I don't want that to be us."

"Agreed. Do you have plans for this weekend? I think I'm ready to go fishing, but I'll need an extra pair of hands."

"I'm off this weekend, unless I get an emergency call. I have to confess, I've never been fishing," Maggie replied.

"You are speaking to the bayou's best fisherman." Sandy chuckled. "I've been fishing ever since I was big enough to hold a cane pole. I catch catfish and take them to LB's for processing. He buys any I can bring in. It's been a side hustle for me since I was little."

"I'll gladly be your second pair of hands. What time?"

"The earlier the better, but nine will do," Sandy replied.

"I'm an early riser, so if earlier is better that's fine with me."

"I'll see you early Saturday morning then. Breakfast is on me, so come hungry."

†

Sandy had battled through injuries before, but nothing that could have prepared her for the intense pain and effort it took to begin to use her arm and hand again. The external wounds had healed well, but Sandy had found she had lost most of the strength in her hand. On her first day of therapy, Maggie came in to check on her.

Sandy could feel the beads of sweat forming on her forehead as she completed the repetitions of the finger exercises the therapist had assigned her. Sandy looked up to find Maggie watching her.

"This is much harder than I thought it would be."

"You've got to be patient with your progress. You can't expect to take the bandages off and immediately return to normal. I know you're not afraid of the hard work, but it's going to be slow before you regain your strength." Maggie placed a comforting hand on Sandy's shoulder.

"You know, patience isn't one of my better qualities." Sandy curled her fingers as tightly as she could. "The pinky isn't going to work again, is it?"

"Probably not much, but it's the best I could do, with what Bubba Gump left me to work with," Maggie replied. "I think you're doing great for your first day. How's the pain?"

"It's about an eight out of ten, but I'll gut through it," Sandy replied through gritted teeth.

"I can order something mild for pain if you need it?" Maggie offered.

Sandy shook her head. "No thanks, Doc, I can handle this."

"Promise me you'll let me know if you can't?"

"I will. Will you be free for lunch after my torture session?"

"I have surgery at two, so yes. My treat in the cafeteria? They cook awesome fried chicken on Wednesdays and you need protein," Maggie replied.

"I've got ten more minutes before I can escape. Betty has already given me instructions for my home exercises."

Maggie looked at Sandy. "I know you are anxious to use that hand, but please let me caution you. Overdoing the home exercises, or trying to use it too soon before you are ready, can be as destructive as not doing your work to get better."

"How do you know me so well?" Sandy asked.

"I see the passion for what you do in your eyes, and nothing lights them up more than talking about working with Cam and your sisters."

"Well, you're wrong about that." Sandy smirked.

"Oh, how so?" Maggie asked.

"You light them up. Every time I see you or think of you, I can feel the glow in them. Cam sees it, too."

"I do believe that's one of the sweetest things I've heard come out of your mouth, Ms. St. Angelo."

†

The first night they shared together seemed magical to Sandy. Unable to use her left arm, she felt awkward, but Maggie didn't appear affected at all. They had finished a steak dinner out on the island, and were cleaning the kitchen when Sandy wrapped her arms around Maggie's waist and began kissing her neck. When Maggie turned in her arms, Sandy saw the desire in her eyes. She kissed her deeply, and when Maggie broke the kiss, she jumped onto the kitchen counter. She pulled Sandy in for a passionate kiss and helped Sandy remove the shorts and panties she wore. Desire took over from there, and Sandy removed the remainder of Maggie's clothes and slowly explored Maggie's body with her hand and mouth. Sandy's tongue teased Maggie's center, causing her to squirm on the counter until she took a handful of Sandy's hair and guided her to the spot throbbing for attention. Maggie's moans filled the cabin, and when Sandy's mouth closed around her clit, Maggie cried out in passion.

After Maggie's breathing slowed, Sandy scooped her off the counter and led her into the bedroom as a storm approached. The rain had begun to fall, tapping on the tin roof as lightning lit the sky. Maggie slowly undressed Sandy, and they made love late into the night.

As Maggie snuggled into her warmth, Sandy chuckled. "I don't think I'll ever look at that kitchen counter again without smiling."

"I love you, Little Tiger," Maggie said.

Sandy smirked at her use of the new nickname given to her for bringing in Bubba Gump. "This Little Tiger loves you, too, and you sure know how to make her purr."

Sandy listened to the sound of the rain, the soft snoring Maggie made as she slept, and her imagination began to soar. Amite had settled in at the end of the bed and Willow stood guard in her bed at the door. She fell asleep dreaming of the house they would build together and the life they would share.

†

To celebrate Sandy completing her therapy, Cam booked an all-woman cruise for them. Luce, Wanda, Liz, Sandy, Maggie, and Cam enjoyed a week-long adventure. On the last night of the cruise, Sandy surprised Maggie with a ring and marriage proposal.

They were up on the top deck with the moon shining across the water when Sandy turned to Maggie. She knelt before her and looked up at Maggie as she opened the ring box. "I know we haven't been together long, but deep in my heart I believe we were drawn together by my injury. I would be very proud if you would say yes to becoming my wife and partner."

Maggie's emerald eyes filled with tears. She nodded. "I would love to be your wife and partner."

When they met the others for breakfast the following morning, Sandy nodded to Cam. She had talked to Cam about her plans to propose to Maggie, and Cam had given her blessing and encouragement.

"I'd like to make an announcement," Sandy said when everyone was seated around the table. She took Maggie's hand in hers. "She said 'yes'."

"That's fantastic news," Liz replied. "Sisters, we have a wedding to plan," she said, rubbing her hands together excitedly.

"Slow your roll, Liz. We haven't even discussed a date yet," Sandy teased. She looked at Cam. "There are two things I need to ask of you. First, will you stand beside me on our special day?"

"Hell, yes, I will," Cam replied. "What else?"

"I'd like permission to build a house for us on the property."

Cam shook her head. "You don't need permission for that. It's your home. Where were you thinking?"

Sandy grinned. "Next to the old oak that has the treehouse we built together. I hope maybe one day we'll have a little one who enjoys it as much as I did."

"That sounds perfect," Cam said, wiping a tear from her eye. She looked at Luce with a smile. "We have some news to share as well. Now that we are legally making our 'alternative fuel,' Luce has decided to switch to reserve status and work with us full time."

"That's great news," Wanda said. "Will we move forward building a cook shack on the homestead?"

"I think it would make life easier for all of us to be closer to home," Cam said with a nod.

Liz cleared her throat. "Just promise me one thing. That we will never lose times like these that we all celebrate together?"

Cam nodded. "I promise we will plan at least one vacation each year together."

The wedding was a small, family event, just as Maggie and Sandy requested, but the homestead was beautifully decorated and the feast afterward was in true St. Angelo style. As the sun began to sink, Maggie looked at Sandy. "We need to head to Baton Rouge soon. Our flight leaves early in the morning."

Cam walked out with them. "I hope you have a great honeymoon. Enjoy the time you have together and cherish the love you have created. We'll see you in a week."

Maggie climbed in behind the wheel and held Sandy's hand gently as they sang country melodies all the way to Baton Rouge. When Sandy closed the door behind them at the hotel, Maggie spun in Sandy's arms. "You have made me a very happy woman today. I look forward to waking up beside you for the rest of our lives."

Sandy's eyes were wet with tears. "I am so proud to call you, my wife." She leaned in for a deep kiss.

"Let's get out of these clothes. I can't wait to devour every inch of you," Maggie teased as she slid the belt from around Sandy's waist.

Maggie had rented a private home on the beach in Cancun for their honeymoon and they spent their days lounging by the pool or in the ocean and their nights walking the beach and making love. On their fourth night, after exhausting themselves making love, Maggie curled up in Sandy's arms. The sounds of the waves breaking against the seawall filled the night.

"This has been such a perfect trip. I wish it never had to end," Maggie said.

"This is only our beginning. I promise we will travel and share many more days like these," Sandy said.

Maggie fell silent for a few minutes and Sandy thought she had fallen asleep. She reached down to pull the covers over them and Maggie's green eyes sparkled up at Sandy. "How would you feel about having a baby? Not right away, but soon?"

"Are you serious? I would love it," Sandy said. "I was hoping one day we would share a child together. There's nothing in this world that I would love more than our child."

"I'll start doing some research when we get back to work," Maggie replied. "I love you Little Tiger."

"I love you most, Doc."

†

When they flew into Baton Rouge, Sandy had planned a side trip. She wanted to take Maggie to Duke's for dinner. "You have never eaten oysters this good. I promise."

Sandy smiled brightly when they entered the restaurant and she looked over at the oyster bar. "Hey, Marcus," she said and threw up her hand in a wave.

The older man looked up to see Sandy and a grin broke out on his face. "Well, if it ain't the Little Tiger. I was hoping you and Cam would stop in sometime."

"We're just coming off our honeymoon, Marcus, I'd like to introduce you to my wife, Maggie."

"It's a great pleasure to meet you, ma'am," Marcus said. "You ready for some oysters?"

"A dozen raw for starters before we tackle the grilled?" Sandy asked.

"I'll be right over. You mind telling me the Little Tiger story. I heard he was twenty feet long and over a ton."

Maggie chuckled. "See the word does get around."

"Yes, ma'am, she was a legend before helping rescue our community after the flood, but her reputation grew immensely when we heard about the Little Tiger of Morganza. I knew right away it was you. Take a seat and I'll be right over."

Two hours and five dozen oysters later, Maggie and Sandy decided to head for home. Sandy asked Marcus for a check and he smiled and shook his head. "My wedding present to you two. Congratulations and take good care of each other. Don't forget to come back and see this old man from time to time."

"Thank you so much. I will guarantee we will be back. Those oysters were fabulous."

When they arrived at the homestead, Sandy pulled to a stop at the top of the driveway. "Home at last. It won't be long until our house is finished and we can start creating our home."

"I love you," Maggie said.

"I love you most."

Cam saw the headlights and rushed out to welcome them home. "I'm glad you made it safely and I hope you had a great trip."

"It was awesome and Marcus sends his regards. We had an early dinner at Duke's."

Cam looked at Maggie. "Aren't those the best oysters you've ever eaten?"

"Yes, without a doubt. I hope we go there again soon."

"I've been promising Luce a trip to Baton Rouge, so maybe we can make a weekend of it."

"Sounds great, Cam. It's good to be home."

†

The first attempt of artificial insemination was unsuccessful. Sandy was disappointed for Maggie, but Maggie had warned her that the first attempt often failed. As soon as she was able, Maggie went in for a second procedure. Sandy stood beside her during the process, holding her hand tightly. Later, as they drove home, she turned to Maggie. "Don't ask me how I know, but we just made a baby."

Maggie kissed Sandy's hand as she drove. "I pray you are right."

A few weeks later, Maggie's examination revealed she was indeed pregnant. Sandy was ecstatic when she heard the news.

"I know you are excited, too, but would you mind if we waited to make an announcement? I don't want anything jinx this."

Sandy nodded. "I know, I was thinking the same thing."

"Get out of my head." Maggie laughed.

CHAPTER TEN

Sandy and Maggie built a beautiful home, and during the family housewarming party, they announced Maggie was pregnant and would give birth in November.

"It will be great to have a little one running around again," Karen said. "The boys constantly remind me they aren't babies anymore." She grinned and ruffled Billy's hair.

When the family left, and it was just the four of them, Luce looked at Cam. "I've been thinking of something that I'd like to discuss, especially after tonight's great news."

Cam leaned forward. "Go ahead."

"Memaw loves it here, and I worry about her getting up in age and living alone. Would it be possible for her to move here with us to help around? She loves babies and could care for the new baby once he or she arrives."

"She," Maggie said. "We're having a baby girl, but you two are the only ones who know. I love the idea of having a reliable babysitter when we both have to return to work."

"Memaw could live with us." Cam said.

"Nope, our place is bigger, and it makes sense to have her here with us," Sandy said.

"Thank you. I'm not sure I can convince Memaw to move, but I'm going to try."

"Let's go talk to her this weekend. November will be here soon." Cam grinned.

Luce nodded. "Thank you all. She's important to me."

"She's family," Sandy said, "and always welcome. There will be plenty of things to keep her busy. She can garden, help with preparing mash for shine, and other routine chores so she won't be sitting idle."

"That will be a huge selling point. Memaw loves her garden," Luce replied.

"Speaking of shine," Cam said. "We've got a busy day tomorrow with a large Texas order we need to fill, so we're going to head home." She winked at Sandy. "We have plans to make for the arrival of this baby girl."

EPILOGUE

Sandy was an emotional wreck the entire gator season as she awaited the birth of their daughter. She'd spent hours talking with Cam, worried she wouldn't know what to do to raise a child. Cam continued to reassure her that each one was different, but they would learn as they go.

When the season finally ended, Sandy spent a week with Maggie, who was just as eager to give birth. Memaw had moved in with them and helped Sandy and Maggie decorate the nursery. They were unable to hide the gender from the rest of the family and soon the nursery was filled with baby girl items.

When Sandy ran over to Cam and Luce's home in the middle of the night to let Cam know Maggie was in labor, Cam grabbed her keys. "I'm driving. There's no way I'm letting this baby be born in a ditch. Grab your bags, and we'll be right over.

After ten long hours, Camille Vincent St. Angelo was born. When Sandy brought her into the room to meet the clan, she had tears running down her face. "Camille, I'd like you to meet your family. Ladies, I give you Camille Vincent St. Angelo, the future all-American shortstop for LSU."

"I'm so happy you named her after Mama. She'll grow up to be a strong, independent woman," Wanda said.

Sandy handed the baby to Cam and she smiled, wrapping her tiny fingers around Cam's pinky. Cam looked up at Sandy. "She's beautiful, and perfect."

When they came home from the hospital, everyone doted on Camille. Memaw was a natural with the infant, and Sandy was a fantastic parent. The businesses continued to thrive, and the family wanted for nothing.

Camille was a month old when Sandy asked Cam to become her godmother. "There's no one on this earth that I would trust my daughter with if something were to happen with Maggie and me," she told Cam.

"I'd be honored, and you know the entire family would help to raise her the right way, but you and Maggie will be around to watch her grow into a beautiful young woman."

Sandy opened a beer bottle and passed it to Cam. "I think you did a pretty decent job raising me."

A tear slid down Cam's cheek. "You remember the story I told you when you were still my little Squirt, about footprints?"

"Yes, that's always been one of my fondest memories of you."

"For many years, our paths were joined as you followed behind me. You were a great softball player, are a great gator hunter, the Little Tiger to be exact, and now an excellent parent. You are the best fisherman I've ever met. But now, instead of following in my footprints, you walk beside me, creating a path of your own, and I'm still just as proud to call you my best friend."

ABOUT ALI SPOONER

Ali Spooner lives in beautiful northwest Florida with her long-term partner and several fur babies. Ali's writing began as a hobby, and with the assistance of the Affinity Rainbow Publishing team has advanced her love of storytelling to a new level.

Ali's characters are primarily everyday people, from cowgirls to psychics. Ali also has created a few supernatural characters in her paranormal series. Several of her twenty-plus books have been Amazon-rated number one choices and always include a happily ever after. Ali's hobbies include photography, reading, travel, college sports, and spending time with family and friends.

OTHER BOOKS IN THE SERIES FROM AFFINITY

Diamond Dreams by Ali Spooner

Cameron St. Angelo dreams of playing softball in the College World Series. Earning a scholarship to play ball for her beloved LSU, brings Cam one-step closer to achieving this dream. When Cam arrives on campus, she joins a family of women who share her love of the sport, and she realizes there is room in her life for another love. This is the beginning of a four-part story, of Cam and the St. Angelo family's struggle to survive in the bayous of South Central Louisiana.

Gator Girlz by Ali Spooner

In the sequel to *Diamond Dreams* Cam St. Angelo finished her freshman year on a high. Her softball career is on path and her lover, Tab Fortner, is planning on spending some time in the bayou with Cam's family before starting their next year of college. Everything seems to fall in place for Cam and Tab as the new school year and softball season take off. All too soon, unfortunate events at the home front, force Cam to leave collage and her softball dreams behind. As always, it's family first.

True North by Ali Spooner

Cam's story continues as the Gator Girlz business continues to thrive under her leadership, but will self-doubt jeopardize her relationship when Bugsy reveals the family moonshine business to an unsuspecting Luce? Will a devastating injury to Sandy end her career as a gator hunter or will it open a door to love? Join the St. Angelo family for a third adventure to find out more about life, loving and family in Bayou Country

.

Affinity
Rainbow Publications

eBooks, Print, Free eBooks

Visit our website for more publications available online.

www.affinityrainbowpublications.com

Published by Affinity Rainbow Publications
A Division of Affinity eBook Press NZ LTD
Canterbury, New Zealand

Registered Company 2517228